G R JORDAN

# Surface Tensions

First published by Carpetless Publishing in 2017

Copyright © G R Jordan, 2017

All rights reserved. No part of this publication may be reproduced, stored, or transmitted in any form or by any means, electronic, mechanical, photocopying, recording, scanning, or otherwise without written permission from the publisher. It is illegal to copy this book, post it to a website, or distribute it by any other means without permission.

Second Edition

ISBN: 978-1-912153-09-1

This book was professionally typeset on Reedsy.
Find out more at reedsy.com

# Contents

| | |
|---|---|
| Dedication | i |
| Something's in the Water | 1 |
| Nature Shoot | 9 |
| Killer's Return | 16 |
| Life Saver | 22 |
| Unexpected Caller | 29 |
| Murdo & Laura | 38 |
| You can Lead a Horse… | 48 |
| Down the Town | 57 |
| A Ministerial Visit | 66 |
| James | 76 |
| Mermaid Hunting | 85 |
| Aftermath | 94 |
| Catching Your Man | 102 |
| Handling the Livestock | 112 |
| Private Pool | 121 |
| Ignition | 129 |
| Riot | 138 |
| Crisis | 145 |
| A New Man on the Scene | 154 |
| A New Place to Swim | 163 |
| The Town Meeting | 172 |
| Hunting Party | 181 |

| | |
|---|---|
| Narrowing of the Sights | 188 |
| Captured | 198 |
| Mrs McKinney's Rescue | 207 |
| Reflection | 218 |
| More from the Author | 225 |
| Acknowledgements | 229 |
| Author Bio | 230 |

# Dedication

To Ken, for your help and support with making my books

# 1

# Something's in the Water

The white trail of the wake was clearly visible in the moonlight, plotting the track back to the mainland port they had left. Tonight the water was barely moving, the odd little reflection of light highlighting the gentlest of oscillations. The familiar salty smell of the sea was caught up in the spray and the breeze generated by the boat's forward motion sent a light chill across his neck.

Decked out in luminous fatigues and topped with an orange plastic hard hat, Donald saw this night as playing out so many others since he had started as a deck hand on the ferries. Twenty-four hours, back and forward, the boat sailed, carrying the many islanders who needed to exert some influence on the mainland. In the summer it was packed with tourists seeking the peace and quiet of the rural locality and who, ironically, tended to break up that perceived nirvana.

It was Donald's habit on the night crossing to stand outside once the port duties had been done. Many colleagues went for a quick kip or sat with a coffee in the rest room. After knowing each other for so long, he had found the banter paled at the later hours and his time was better employed in a restful reflection of the sea or in quiet conversation with his maker. Tonight the waters were providing therapy.

Donald found it funny how at night you would sometimes see things in the water. Devious creatures of the deep would raise their heads only to be a gull sat on the waves, or a buoy calmly marking the creel locations. Occasionally, the dolphins or porpoises would be leaping and he would watch with awe how they sleekly slid through the churning waves or jumped out from the flat watery tableau.

Tonight was quiet in the extreme for he had seen nothing at all. Iain, the new, young deckhand, had ventured out for a cigarette beside him. Apparently the national side had lost the football which deserved a spit on the floor in disgust. Smoking stank but Iain was good company otherwise. They had had a muttered conversation about the new rosters and annual leave and then stood in silence until the bright tip of Iain's cigarette had finally run out of fuel. If only he'd get one of those e-cigarettes, Donald had thought.

Donald ventured inside to the rest room to pick up a coffee, loaded with two sugars and a bucket of milk. It was strong and thick regardless and a requirement on these cold nights on deck. For all his career on the boat, he had had trouble with the night-shifts. Constantly that dragging desire to sleep would come to him and he would force it away with a walk, a little cool air or a monumental blast of caffeine. He had tried going to his bed between dockings but he always felt worse for the little sleep he got. No, he was better having a proper sleep after his shift was over.

Sunday tomorrow, he thought. Mum would be leaving for the little church just before twelve, to go and sing her psalms. She'd been wearing that hat she had bought at the local shop, just a little ostentatious, and a black skirt and white shirt. Immaculate in all her clothes, his Mum was always harassing him to come with her. Not that she had ever been that polite before his Dad had died.

He remembered those days of being hauled out of bed and thrown into the bath. On emerging spotless, he had had to put on his Sunday suit, black with a black tie. It doubled for funerals as well which were another formal occasion he grew up hating. Then he would have to sit around, either listening to his father droning on from that bible or remaining in silence.

The bible was large, nowadays you would say just shy of A4, and in the King James. His Dad had always said it was the correct translation and the book had held a prominent place on the mantelpiece over the fire. Then he would be dragged along with his sister to the church. He remembered the wooden pews, cold and unforgiving as the message was thundered out at him from the pulpit. Colourless, dispassionate and without love he always thought. Twice they would go on a Sunday and by the evening, he knew he was lousy at this Godly life.

But he had survived the wrath of his parents quite well, unlike his sister. Or "that disgrace of a sister of yours" as she was also known. Mairi had been born with a fantastic figure. All through school he had heard the other boys talk of his older sister and what she would do for you. Many dreams of passionate nights had been recounted before him and he had found it hard to retain an accurate view of her.

She had gone to university much to their parent's disgust, studying the arts, photography and graphic media in particular. Mairi's photos were fantastic, evocative and life affirming but the subject matter often offended her Mum and Dad. Nudity in any sense, or more accurately flesh, was offensive to a generation brought up on full coverage clothing.

Then Dad had died. Just dropped one day. Heart attack. To be fair, he was eighteen stone and had rarely exercised. The whole village had been out. And out to get Mairi, it seemed. Daughter who had brought shame, who had walked astray. Donald had felt for her sister for their Mum had also given her a cold shoulder.

Mairi continued at the university but money was short. So she had turned to use her body for some pictures in a magazine. It was a lad's magazine and she wasn't mentioned by name, just in the background, poolside, lounging on an inflatable bed attended by a minor celebrity. There was outrage from home. But Donald had known the whole story. Mairi had insisted she wouldn't go topless, even when asked at the shoot and other girls had agreed. But that counted for nothing. As far as Mum was concerned, she was in the devil's world and she could stay there.

Donald was happy standing outside on such a clear, if cold night, with nothing to annoy him except the odd seagull's cry. It was funny how they followed the boat, especially at night when there was usually only the odd smoker or himself on the ferry. It was doubtful that even if they managed to land next to those puffers that a drag would be forthcoming.

A glimpse of something caught his eye. A tail had flicked out of the water and dived back down quickly. Now, this was something. Dolphins, or even the porpoises, were a joy to watch. A bit like penguins at the zoo, you could never tear yourself away while they were up to their antics. Walking to the handrail on the ship's edge, he scoured the sea. The moonlight caught the tail of something rolling into the water.

It was harder at night to see what was going on but with

how calm it was, at least the disturbances in the surface were showing quite readily. There was another one. And another. Donald chastised himself. He was seeing them late, never catching the front, never a nose or top fin. They also seemed quite large too, certainly close to that of an average person.

Now that was unusual. There was definitely a tinge of yellow with that one. No, not yellow, blonde. Bizarre. Something must have been caught around its nose. Certainly, Donald was not aware of any blonde markings on the dolphins. He wasn't as sure about the porpoises but the creatures were surely too big for porpoises.

Then there was a red streak followed by the tail. This was just wrong, thought Donald. I must be knackered. It was only the second night of a two week stint but sometimes this was the time when you were most close to sleep, not having adjusted your pattern yet. There again, red. And that one, could that have been a dark brown hue he saw? Time for another cuppa, Donald decided.

Inside the ship, Donald headed down to the crew only corridor and into the canteen. James, the young lad only on his second trip, was there to serve the crew and seemed far too cheery for this time of night.

"Evening Donald, what can I get you this fine night?"

"Coffee, James, thank you. Good and strong, mind. Feeling a wee bit bushed at the moment."

"Very good. You're the only one up and about except for the upper decks. Rest of the deck crew have gone for their nap. I usually get some of my book read about this time."

"Don't let me stop you. Don't know how you read this time of night. It'd put me to sleep. Nothing on the telly at all?"

"Another rerun of that tosser who gives advice to drop-outs

who want to be on the telly with their issues. Or there's some foreign crap about meditation and chanting. Crack-heads by the look of it."

"Live and let live, James. If it keeps them happy." Installed at a fixed chair with table in front, Donald settled down to enjoy his coffee.

There was something joyous about night shifts, something that touched Donald's core. With the rest of the world asleep, you got to see it in a more peaceful state. Generally, night workers were more convivial and managers were absent from the daily routine.

It seemed to Donald that managers got in the way in this life. When you had purpose or a job to do then you got on with it. You didn't need someone to oversee you and to keep track. Knowing what needed done, how to do it and when it was required, all lead to a tidy and useful job being completed. Managers got in the way with paperwork and reports. Waste of space generally. Designated for people who couldn't do the job in the first place.

Fortunately enough, his captain wasn't a manager. He was thorough, let his crew know the score and then expected it completed. Yes, he wasn't bad at all. As long as he didn't know about the strange sightings of colours in the sea. Donald laughed. He'd be confined to his room like that.

Donald's thoughts turned to fishing. After this tour on the ship he'd take some days down at the rocks near the shoreline to cast a few. If the sun was out, there was nothing to beat hunting the mackerel with a feather line, hoping that he could escape the machinations of those pesky seals. Beautiful creatures in their own right but damn pests near the line.

Coffee consumed, Donald acknowledged James and headed

back out onto the rear deck. He breathed in the sea air and settled in his stance to watch the wake again, letting his mind wander through various ideas he had about purchasing a poly tunnel this summer. Then something caught his eye.

At first he thought it was those flecks of colour on the dolphins he had struggled to attribute. But he couldn't see any dolphins. There was however a blonde patch of what looked like hair. Probably a straw mat or something, cast aside by some non-ecotourist. However, as the water lapped by it, a face was obvious. Donald blinked hard but then it was gone. I told James a strong coffee, he thought.

Then there was a red mat. Bizarre that there should be two soo close, unless some ship lost a box of wigs or something. That would be it. Just some silly jetsam causing mischief in the night. This would have been an adequate explanation except he saw another face under the red wig. Dolls or mannequins, that's it. Hang on, Donald chastised himself, that one's waving.

Sure enough an arm had come out of the water and was waving in fashion towards him. Dumbfounded, all Donald could do was to wave back. Suddenly the wig disappeared and he swore he had seen a large fish tail whip up behind the wig and disappear into the waves.

Half in disbelief and half in wonder, Donald continued to stare at the now empty piece of water where the face had been. All thoughts of fishing or the poly tunnel were gone as he debated whether he had begun to lose his mind. Confused, he strode over to the railing on the deck-side.

There was nothing at all. Just the lap of the sea and the wake eternally marking the ship's path. Good, thought Donald, just a bad night, I'm just tired. A decent bit of kip and I'll be right as rain.

Without warning, no more than fifty meters away, a black-haired head popped out of the sea. Donald drew his breath in sharply as he saw a face stare up at him. It was pale in the extreme but was very human in aspect. There were two sleek, black eyebrows, dark, deep-set eyes, drawn cheek bones and pale lips. Unlike the roundness of all other heads he knew this one had more of a keel's look to it. The nose was prominent and the culminating point of the face, giving a slipperiness through the water, Donald surmised.

His hand held onto the rail preventing him from buckling but his heart was pounding. He'd heard old sailor's tales of mermaids but no one these days ever took it seriously. Still, right in front of him was a woman in the sea who had the ability to swim alongside this ship at speed and maintain her head above water. It had to be a mermaid. No human could do this.

The creature started to sing. She, if indeed it was a she, had the depth of panpipes but the tone of lark when in voice. Like all birdsong, it was clear in its call and Donald wondered if this was some sort of mating call, not that it ever occurred to him that he may be the victim. He wallowed in the song, transfixed by the voice and the excitement of this discovery.

A red and a blonde haired pair joined her and they sang together, like the most harmonious organ the world has heard. Side by side and then interchanging, they trailed the ship with their show occasionally dipping back beneath the waves. And then with no warning they dived to the deep, leaving a happily bemused but pondering Donald to his own devices.

# 2

# Nature Shoot

Kiera enjoyed these sorts of days, the kind which although cold and crisp, allowed you to be out and about with Mother Nature. There was nothing to beat walking over the dunes with only a light wind giving a small chill to your face. As the day wore on, you'd be able to embrace the heat from the sun, albeit pitiful compared to the summer's day.

The other reason these days were her favourite was the light. Grey days with the drizzle and murk made getting a decent shot so very difficult and although her cameras were of a decent quality, they were hardly truly professional. All the filters, batteries, cards and attachments cost money, something that this artistic photographer looking to progress beyond amateur status did not possess.

She did have the canvas though. The island was a source of inspiration, beauty and chaos. The changeable weather constantly altered the scenery and the variety of animal life pushed her talents to their limits. But without doubt, the best contrast came with the people. Ranging from the grey pallor of fixated religious types through to eccentric foreigners, exploring their freedom in the wilds, all life seemed to migrate to this last stop before the ocean.

Not that all was sweetness and light. Kiera had gotten into trouble recently for daring to take pictures of a funeral. She had been fascinated by the large turnout in the village, the division between those who saw fit to wait outside the church and those inside, and then by the bleak and monochrome procession to the windswept graveyard. There was an unwritten structure broken by some men smoking fags outside the church, cursory nods to the coffin and loose connections. A Dubliner by birth, Kiera was keenly aware she was not part of the funeral despite having known the deceased and having asked her permission to shoot the funeral days before her friend's medically predicted demise.

Little was said, no obvious words telling her to desist, but the overall ambience was one of not being wanted. She didn't care though as Christine, her departed friend, would have loved the exposures. Many times Chrissy had laughed at her own culture, sharing with Kiera its little foibles, as Kiera told of the sillier side of Dublin. She wondered sometimes how many of those at the funeral really knew her friend's thoughts.

Such thoughts were not going to stop her enjoyment of the day and she continued her dandering towards the rocky outcrop that would now be exposed, it being low tide. Hopefully, the rock pools would yield a few trapped sea creatures for her to try the new macro-lens purchased from the internet a mere week ago. The smallest of creatures fascinated her with the micro worlds they lived in. Even as a child visiting the beach back home in Ireland, she had investigated these trapped communities with her grandfather. He would kneel on the corner of the pools occasionally disturbing the water with a single finger hoping to prod something into life. Nowadays she thought of herself prodding a finger through her photographs hoping to provoke a reaction from the locals.

That's strange, thought Kiera, there's someone down there already sat on the rocks. Is she topless? Flippin' heck she is. She'd catch chill out here today, it's not like it's the height of summer.

The girl in question had her back to Kiera but was sporting long, curled and tangled hair. Clearly the morning grooming routine of the brush had not be applied and the hair was at least damp if not wet. The blonde curls sat on the backdrop of bare shoulders, two bony blades marking the top of her back which was extremely pale. Not that this was surprising in this weather. With a photographer's eye for detail, Kiera also spotted that the skin, although a milky white colour, also had waxiness to it, like Vaseline had been rubbed over it. Ah, thought Kiera, maybe it's goose fat to fight the cold water. But who the hell's going to go top off for a swim today?

Kiera was slightly built with dark brown hair. Being only just over five foot tall, she was well hidden by the dunes she was emerging from. Always light on her feet, Kiera was about to call out to the girl when she noticed something peculiar about her.

At first she thought the girl was wearing turquoise bottoms and rather large encompassing ones at that. However, on getting closer, Kiera had to clasp her mouth with her hand as she saw a tail, similar to that of a fish, starting at her hips. They say first impressions last but Kiera's brain reacted quickly looking around for a film crew or camera person. Surely this must be a shoot or something.

Kiera was about to acknowledge her presence but then thought if they were shooting, she may cause a disturbance. So she went down to her haunches to await developments. The tail fascinated her as the detail was incredible. The scales looked immaculate and even had the impression of water sitting on them. The little curve in the top middle of the tail had the smallest pooling evident and when the tail flicked the motion was seamless. A gentle splat was heard on each occasion as the tail caught a small rock pool.

Amazed at the detail of the work, Kiera kept calm and enjoyed the obvious modelling in progress. She started to wonder how they had gotten permission for this, with no marshallers or signs to prevent anyone from walking into the area. There was also no reflecting boards or camera equipment evident. Maybe, she thought, the photographer was shooting from distance for a scenery shot. Maybe she wasn't topless either but had clam shells over her extremities thus not offending the religious section of the island.

Still something was bothering Kiera and she couldn't put her finger on it. Sure, this was somewhat bizarre but wasn't all photography when you were forcing a picture. Nature was always much more accommodating.

That was it, just below the ears. There were gills. Admittedly she was at a distance but they looked incredible. Kiera picked up her camera and zoomed in with her telescopic lens so that the gill filled her viewer. It was astonishing. There were no join marks at all. It must have been synthetic rubber or something but to look so perfect through a lens was beyond any make-up she had seen previously.

Moving the camera down the girl's back, Kiera saw the flesh slowly change into scales of the tail, again without any major blemishes. The work was truly outstanding. Hats off to this crowd, thought Kiera, and doing it out here in the open.

Whilst studying the girl's back, she saw her turn and Kiera dropped the camera down. Looking straight at her was a frightened face with transfixed eyes. There was a degree of strangeness about the visage, straight on, looking rather narrow. The one thing not in doubt was the fear of the girl as her shoulders were trembling and her hands shaking.

"It's okay love. Just walking past. Love that wonderful outfit. So good it looks real. I'd be careful though dressing like that on top, some round here can be a bit funny. Oh, not like in perverted way, although I guess everywhere's got them, but it'll be an affront to the more religious ones." Dammit, thought Kiera, if I looked that good I'd model like that too. She laughed a little inside at the thought. She'd never be brave enough for that.

The girl spoke. Well "spoke" was inaccurate as she made a sound rather like the ones dolphins make. Not the short gibbering sounds but the longer honk rather similar to a gull. She's nothing if not in character. Kiera strode forward now to shake the girl's hand realising she was quite an actress.

The girl panicked and rolled hard off the rock into the sea. Kiera watched aghast, stunned at the speed of the girl in the water. Then the instinct kicked in and she raised her camera to shoot. The girl was disappearing fast but her tail could be seen popping in and out of the water. Kiera clicked off maybe a dozen shots and then she was gone.

Slowly, Kiera dropped the camera from her eye and stood quietly gazing at the sea in front of her. It was rolling in gently and breaking small white waves onto the rocks. Scanning the beach she could see no sign of anyone else. The hairs on the back of her neck stood up as she drew her conclusion.

Mermaid, a real life mermaid. The voice, that bizarre sound

that a human would have such difficulty in reproducing. Her tail so resplendent and incredibly functional in the water. No person could swim like that, even with flippers. And then there was the total abandon with which she had sat there, unclothed, like she didn't even know it was an issue. Like a toddler with a descending nappy.

Kiera was bewildered at what to do next. Should she run and tell someone? No, not without evidence she thought and spun her camera to the rear to check her photos in the view screen. One by one she ran through each shot which differed by just a fraction from the first. Some had just sea in them but some of the others had a dark image in the water. Using the functions of the camera, she blew each of these images up and refined it. There was a tail, the detail which was remarkably good, the overlaying of the scales and slight distortion of colour due to the angle of the sun. Throughout the sequence the tail had a variation of exposure above the water but none of the pictures had the one thing she needed, flesh.

Kiera wondered who she could tell, who would believe her. No one was her conclusion and she decided that she would need to go mermaid hunting. But how and where? Maybe the remoteness of this point had caused the mermaid to come ashore. Was it the crashing water on the rocks, giving an almost spa effect? Surely it wasn't food? What did mermaids eat anyway? Could she lure one out?

A bona fide photograph would sell for a fortune, pondered Kiera, and she could use the money. It wasn't like the landscapes were bringing in a lot. No, it would need to be a hunt under the radar. She would be like one of David Attenborough's cameramen, stalking the lesser spotted anteater near the Amazon jungle. Okay, a little bit cooler and with a pub at the end of the day but something like that. Best to keep it all in until I can get a full on picture.

Departing the beach at a pace, Kiera headed home to plan her tracking strategy and to dream of a National Geographic front cover.

# 3

# Killer's Return

"That's the last of them, Iain lad, you can take a break now. I'll just take her round into the cove at the wee island. We can rip into those sandwiches your mother made and get a wee dram of the good stuff too."

Arms aching, Iain McClaren collapsed back into the small boat. What had possessed his Uncle to get up at this ridiculous hour to pick up some creels? The man was obsessed with the sea state and this afternoon's was "showing a wee bit of a swelly" as his Uncle had put it.

Growing up, trips out with Uncle Seoras had been a joy. Iain had been shown how to fish, could get away from homework, was clear of his mother's purse strings and was allowed to be a man early, getting a wee nip of the finest "special tea" from the age of eight. Being a bachelor, Seoras had treated Iain like a son, but a spoilt one, on account of the tragedy that Iain had witnessed.

It happened fourteen years ago and Iain struggled to remember all the detail of the day. His mother recounted that Iain's father had decided to take Iain away for the weekend, his first trip to the "big smoke" on the mainland. His father had been a keen footballer and decreed his son should be introduced to the main stand of his beloved club to experience a proper pie and the atmosphere. Catching the early morning ferry, they had breakfasted in the canteen area before standing out on deck to see the sun rise.

He remembered his father's words about the man who was standing up on the handrails at the port side of the ship. "Bloody piss head, people like that should be kicked off our wee island." The ship had reached the open sea and it was in a rough state, similar to the man on the rails. The man had been there, singing loudly, and his father had gone to remonstrate with him to come down. Iain could picture a fracas before the man, holding onto his father, had fallen off the side taking his father with him. Then a man had grabbed a life ring and thrown it into the sea. The man had then run off, to find a crew member Iain realised with hindsight, and he had been left alone on the deck. He was able to peek through a hole in the side where the ropes went and saw his father fighting in the waves.

"That's us just about there. Where did you put the whiskey? I think I'll put her alongside the wee jetty and I'll go ashore for a wee kip. You know how I hate to lie on the bench on the boat."

His uncle was a technophobe and someone who was particularly bad at keeping his personal business secret. The island they were about to moor to was only a quarter of a mile wide by six hundred or so yards long but it did contain one small hut, braced down with straps for the frequent strong winds. Iain had been taken there by his uncle but often he was kept away with some excuse or other, always similar to the present one.

Iain took the bottle of whiskey and handed it to his uncle after the boat was tied up. A kip generally meant an hour or two and Iain watched his uncle take his sandwiches and another plastic bag containing some magazines. Officially these were fishing magazines, or possibly something about boats.

One day, at the age of thirteen, Iain had gone looking for his uncle in the hut when he had cut his hand while playing during the time of his uncle's kip. His uncle was in an alcoholic sleep and Iain had found the fishing magazines strangely interesting. He was also stunned how many women seemed to have so few inhibitions around these boats. Obviously they came from warmer climates than the island but Iain had decided boats were the thing to take along with the fairer sex. Rebecca MacKenzie hadn't shared the same excitement when he took her to his uncle's boat two years later.

Having an hour or two to kill was nothing new to Iain and usually he would bring his tablet to watch a recent DVD he had acquired. Today, he had forgotten the tablet due to the early start and thought he might try and regain some of the bed hours he had been forced to forgo. Iain polished off the sandwiches his mother had made to keep any hunger pangs away and then moulded himself up against the side of the boat. Closing his eyes, he tried to think of nothing and drift away.

A splash of water hit his face. Groggily, Iain shook his head. Must have been a fish jumping or something he thought. Glancing at his watch he realised he had been asleep for some forty minutes. Coffee was always a good thing. His mother would pack some oblivious to the fact her brother would never touch it but usually pour out the flask on the beach when returning. Having reached his later teens Iain had started drinking some but could never manage the large flask his mother inevitably made.

He started to get up but fell back down at the sight in front of him. There were three women in the sea about two hundred yards away. Their heads were evident above the water but they would occasionally dive into the water pushing and shoving each other in a frolicking fashion. Their abandon indicated his presence was unnoticed and he kept low peering over the edge of the boat. After a few minutes they were swimming closer to the rocks of the island and the water dipped down to their midriffs. Iain could not believe his eyes staring at his Uncle's boat women come to life.

There were two blonde haired women and one brunette and it was this lady who grabbed his attention. He guessed she was about thirty but her figure was stunning. Every curve screamed out to the young man in him and he fought to keep his composure. This was like one of those sets from a men's magazine, the type you imagine because you know they never come true.

His drooling stares were quickly abated as the women clambered onto the rocks. They were back. He had told people about them, screamed at what they had done but no one had believed him. His mother had refused to hear anything about the tailed women and his uncle had initially told him to keep quiet for his mother's sake. Bad enough for her to lose a husband but to have her boy witter on about mermaids taking him. Such nonsense was too much to deal with.

In the following five years, he remembered how his uncle would hold him by the throat telling him they would lock him up if he didn't give up on this mad tale. It had been ten years since he had spoken to anyone of what he had seen but now it had confronted him again. They would know now, he thought, learn that I was never in shock. They can finally hunt these beasts from the sea.

I'll get my uncle, reasoned Iain. He'll see them and tell everyone. There'll be a hunt, a trawl of the seabed for them. Who am I kidding? He's just a drunk to them. Our words will mean nothing. I'll need a carcass.

All juvenile, erotic ideas purged from his head, Iain sneaked quietly off the boat onto the shore. The mermaids were quietly sitting on the rocks closest the sea, soaking up a little sun. In his mind he saw no perfect skin, no curved beauty, only an evil beast. The rage took hold of him and he selected some moderate sized stones.

Luckily, the mermaids had started to splash up some water over each other and were starting to converse in seal-like calls. Like a hunter smelling blood, Iain cautiously crept towards his prey, having the sense to remain downwind and to choose his steps carefully. Finding a large rock as cover, he knelt down preparing for his assault. If he could hit one in the head and knock it out then he would have at least a body if it didn't come quietly. Breathing deeply, he pictured his father's face drowning in the water, thrashing arms and skin mixed with scales encircling him. They had killed his father, left him with a perverted drunk of an uncle and a mother too steeped in pain to let her son be free. The bitches would pay.

Rising up, he let loose with one stone after another, racing towards his prey. The first two stones hit the brunette mermaid on the shoulders and she howled in pain but immediately rolled off the rock in flight. The other mermaids let loose an ear piercing squeal and immediately propelled themselves into the sea. Iain's third, fourth and fifth stones all fell harmlessly into the water and as he reached the edge of the rocks nothing remained to indicate the presence of the mermaids.

Brooding and once again perched in the bowels of the boat, Iain heard his uncle returning. He barely acknowledged his uncle's arrival causing his relative to give him a gentle kick.

"On your feet slacker," said his uncle, "time to get this catch back to land. Oh, cheer up, give your face a joyride why don't you?"

"Shut up."

"Watch your mouth young man. What's got into you? You were fine this morning."

"Nothing, okay!" Iain's sarcastic tone was not well received.

"Something's up. Go on out with it. What's at ye?"

"It's nothing."

"Bollocks. What's up?"

"Just saw the mermaids again." His uncle's face crimsoned immediately, his shoulders hunching before launching a tirade.

"Just cut that crap out. There's no such thing. You gave your mother enough grief with that nonsense over the years. So don't start, okay? Not a word or I'll crack one off your head for ye. Sweet Mary, ain't it about time you grew up. I'm sorry your dad drowned but that's all that happened. Wanna blame someone, blame that drunk git of a passenger. They picked the wrong one out of the sea that day. Enough Iain, that's all, enough!"

Iain had felt his uncle's fists before and so he got up and started casting off the boat. Idiot, he thought, I'll show him, I'll show them all when I drop a carcass in the town square in front of them all. Time to hunt me a mermaid.

# 4

# Life Saver

"Now Donald, you know they shouldn't be sailing that boat on the Sabbath."

"Yes, Reverend McKinney but they only do a twenty-four seven contract. We are contracted to the boat for the whole two weeks."

"Yes, but they shouldn't sail on our Lord's Day, Donald, you do see that. The sailing is against what the good book says."

"Well, I see what you are saying but either way with me I'm working. Even before the Sunday sailing I was always painting or cleaning up on the Sunday. It wasn't like the shop workers, I never had the day off."

"That's being essential Donald. These Sunday crossings are hardly essential."

Donald cut his losses and shook the large daunting hands of the Reverend McKinney, a man who had watched over his soul from birth. Every Sunday he had gone with his parents to the grey building in the center of the village, morning and evening before stepping forward that Communion Friday and taking the bread and wine the following Sunday. It wasn't that he didn't appreciate his upbringing or indeed his Christian home but he felt constricted at times by the old styles. Many times he had been away on the mainland and had indulged in those "foolish instruments and songs" or had shared where the women had prayed too.

Home was frustrating and Donald was plucking up the courage to tell his mother he would soon be moving out. The familiar but staunch ways were a bind he was unable to live with any longer. His job on the boat gave him two weeks grace at a time but it was hardly living, going back and forth over the sea and he understood his home should be on the mainland. A wee flat, maybe in the city, or maybe a small house in a quiet village with a good bus service. He wasn't searching the high life, merely his life.

Sunday lunch was eaten, lamb with mother's wonderful gravy and, of course, grace beforehand. Thankfulness, he understood but Donald struggled now with routine thanking, was it even acknowledgement at all or mere ritual. When he had taken this up with his father one quiet Sabbath afternoon before he had passed away, there was at first an embarrassed silence before his father clarified, "it's just what we do." That was the problem for Donald at home, little exploration of anything, just a resounding confirmation of the status quo.

Donald told his mother he would take a walk, mentioning Jesus had seen it as a good idea on the Sabbath to quell any dissent. In order to avoid his parent any scandal, he kept well out of sight and clambered down to the hidden shoreline less than a mile from the house. Usually he would meet one of the heathen dog walkers, as she called them, letting the animals do what so many children were denied on their day of rest. Aiden, an Irish catholic on the boat, described how they would all see the hurling or the football on a Sunday after mass in

Ireland. That's Catholics for you, his dad would have said.

It had been two weeks since the incident with the mermaids on the ferry and Donald had come to the conclusion he had seen the equivalent of a mirage. Whilst the event was memorable, it was clearly also an illusion. Part of him praised himself for managing to keep control and not involving the others. The teasing it would have generated would have lasted a good year or two at the minimum and he had had enough flack over some of the church incidents already. The island reverence never seemed to make it off shore.

Working on the boat made relationships hard, thought Donald. He hadn't seen Kiera in a few weeks which bothered him. Since his mother disapproved of her, being Irish, probably catholic and not holding a proper job, just that photography nonsense, Donald had to be quite secretive about their meetings. Since he had got back off the boat four days ago he had been up to her house five times but each time she was out.

The last time they had been together she was so down, still grieving the loss of her friend. Part of him had felt guilty that while she was crying on his shoulder, he had enjoyed her curly, black hair blowing gently in the wind. Despite her mourning, she had still looked gorgeous in her black jeans and red fleece jacket. When they had parted, he had watched her go, admiring her behind and itching for his two week work detail to hurry past. But he believed standing watching was as intimate as he would ever get with Kiera.

It would be risky dropping up on a Sunday as the walk would take him past the Reverend McKinney's manse. Waiting until the evening service was out of the question, as his absence would be noted but maybe a quick drop in would work. Yes, he would, stuff them. Kiera was more important than some auld nosey parker's offended pride. But he would cut up through the high rocks by the beach at the small jetty just to keep out of the way. No point taking unnecessary flak.

Donald almost broke into a skip such was his delight at reaching this rebellious decision. His thoughts turned to wondering what Kiera would be wearing and if she would have her hair loosely tied up or draped down to her shoulders as he preferred it. From the corner of his mind came an idea that Kiera took a bath on a Sunday afternoon as there was so little else to do. Maybe this wasn't a good time to be going. A deviant thought said "oh yes it is" but Donald managed to persuade himself this was a call of necessity to a friend rather than a hopeful romantic encounter. Not that the debate was extensive.

He hadn't been walking slowly but Donald now found himself breaking into a half-run skipping action, taking care around the potholes on the path by the sea. Beside him the rocks were on display with the tide now almost fully out. Little rock pools and crevices where he had played as a child were now ignored at the thought of getting up to Kiera's cottage. The little jetty at the beach came into view as he looked for the sheep trail up past the crofts. Out of the corner of his eye, he saw a colour that didn't seem quite right.

Right at the base of the jetty where it met the rocks, it wasn't unusual to see some netting or plastic washed up. If the object had been bright pink or a deep blue, Donald wouldn't have taken a second glance. But the colour was that of flesh, extremely pale and certainly with a translucent quality, like fish skin. With his second glance, Donald's skin went cold as he saw the top half of a body. Bloody hell he thought, then apologised for swearing.

Taking off at a run, it took Donald a mere ten seconds to get up to the body. It had the subtle curves of a woman with jet black straight hair now matted into the sand. As Donald touched the body, he found it cold and slippery. He rolled the woman over. Ignoring her naked torso, he immediately used his first aid training placing his head to her mouth searching for her breath. There was nothing. Hand grasped round her mouth forcing it open, Donald blew air into the woman's mouth, sharply and with vigour, staring at her chest, searching for any lung function.

There was nothing. Not a sign of life. Several times he tried and felt the water rising up toward him as the tide was turning in. She must be cold, thought Donald. I'll lift her up the beach slightly and try some resuscitation up there. Grabbing her under the armpits, Donald pulled hard dragging the poor woman from water. Then he saw it.

The scaly tail of the mermaid was still showing a blue-green sheen. Donald's heart pounded as he took in the motionless appendage. For a few moments he stopped his rescuing action and stood dumbstruck by the revelation that sea mirages were not his thing. Then his benevolent instinct took over and he hauled the stricken mermaid to a clear area of beach to see if he could render further assistance.

Once again he knelt beside her and checked her chest for signs of breathing. With none present he gripped her nose and blew hard the prescribed times into her mouth before pushing down hard on her chest. After a few minutes action, he checked his patient for signs of life. There was nothing. A quick glance around told him there was no one, not even a Sabbath dog walker on whom to cry out for assistance.

Right, thought Donald, I need to pick up the lady and get to the nearest house. Surely I can find a phone there and get an ambulance. Or a vet. What do you call for a mermaid? One for each end? She does look quite heavy mind. Nothing for it though, emergency situation and all that.

Donald took her hands and straddled over her, attempting to pull the mermaid up towards him. Once he had her vaguely sitting upright, Donald thought he would crouch down placing his shoulder into her stomach. From there he would rock back lifting her up on his shoulder and grabbing her by the tail he would make good progress, holding her like a sack of potatoes.

All was going well, and despite having to work past the mermaid's ample chest, Donald got himself into the brace position ready to lift her onto his shoulder. Accelerating upward she did indeed hook over his shoulder. Attempting to get both hands a hold on her tail, he found it to be incredibly slippery and she sailed right off his shoulder somersaulting onto her back on the sand. Donald scanned the horizon, worried that someone might misconstrue this as cavorting with a topless swimmer.

Despite the ludicrousness of the moment, Donald sensed time was of the essence, noticing the mermaid's scales were starting to lose their sheen. There's nothing for it, he thought. Reaching down, Donald slid an arm under the rear of her tail. He took the mermaids arm and slung it round his neck, sliding his own free arm around her back. Bending his knees he lifted her up, struggling to support her weight.

Right, he decided, to the nearest house. Then the fear struck him. It was a Sunday. Not good to be out here. He was carrying a topless mermaid. There could be some controversy about that. Desperately he sought his biblical knowledge about whether this sort of action was okay. He knew Song of Songs had some raunchy bits but was unsure how they applied in this situation. There was also the bit about pulling your ass out of a pit on a Sunday but was this the same?

Part of Donald cursed himself for this stupid line of thought while he had a potential dead woman on his hands. Ah, the police might be awkward about that too, especially if he mentioned his previous sightings of mermaids. Damn, thought Donald, what do I do? Suddenly an answer came. Whether it was a good answer, an appropriate answer or even a workable answer was a question Donald's brain never had the pleasure of entertaining. Instead, he started his staggering march, similar to the strongman carrying the car shell in those feats of strength competitions. Only one thought was on his mind. Kiera. She'll know what to do. As to Kiera's qualifications for dealing with semi-naked fish women in a state of near death, these were mere details for another time. No, Kiera was the answer. No scandal, no chastisement, no police. Just Kiera.

Donald, now focused, performed one of those herculean moments that all men hope they have inside them and ignored all aches and pains as he haphazardly negotiated the path to Kiera's.

# 5

# Unexpected Caller

Stretching across the bath, she felt the steam reaching the underside of her neck and held her pose for a moment, relishing the warmth. This was going to be sweet. She had the bath bomb all ready, anticipating the splash followed by the dizzying fizz of the pink coloured ball as it sped round the tub. Sundays were made for moments like this. Kiera dropped her robe and prepared to step into the enameled basin.

The sound of the practical but rather drab doorbell broke her perfect moment and even brought forth a little swear word. Kiera's inclination was to ignore the door until she heard the frantic banging of the never used door knocker. Who in their right mind would be giving it lardy on a Sunday afternoon? Well, they were about to get a piece of her mind.

Opening the door she was confronted by an out of breath Donald, face dripping in sweat. In his arms was a topless brunette with a distinctly fishy smell and a dull scaly tail.

"Donald! How the hell did you find the mermaid? What are you doing with her here?"

He barged past, heading straight for the bathroom but she clocked his appreciative glance at her legs and short white gown. By the time she had closed the door and followed, the sound of a splash had been heard. Entering the room, Kiera saw water running across the wooden floor and a mermaid lying, eyes closed, in her bath.

"Warm water," said Donald, "that was good thinking."

"Did you leave any water in the bath?"

"Sorry. Didn't know where to go."

"It's okay, all my male visitors bring their half-naked amphibian girlfriends with them."

"Kiera........Kiera, I think she's dead."

"Dead! You killed her."

Donald looked at Kiera in horror. How could she think such a thing of him?

"No, flippin' heck Kiera, no! She was in the water, just lying. Look at the tail. Look! It's gone dull. Like mackerel when they've died. Lost the colour. I think she's had it."

Kiera leaned over the bath, regardless of her inadequate attire and tried for a pulse at the neck. There was nothing. She tried an arm and again there was nothing. Donald crouched on the floor, looked like a puppy, hoping for a treat but found no hope from its master.

"There's nothing Donald, I'm sorry. Just nothing." Trying to find something to say, Kiera found herself at a loss. Donald was exhausted, totally at a loss and looking for some sort of comfort. All she could do was crouch beside him and place an arm around. She nestled her head on his shoulder and felt his shoulders sharply rise and fall as he fought back tears of exasperation.

"You tried Donald, God love you, you tried." For several minutes she held her embrace before rising. Briefly she left the bathroom to put on a pot of tea, before returning and standing a little aloof from him. While he fought to get back his composure, she busied herself by glancing round the bathroom, anything but looking at the body in the tub. The bright coloured curtains she had worked so hard to put up when the plasterboard would hold no screws. The green and white mat on the floor with its giant shamrock bought by friends from the university she had attended. Then the small hippo that squirted water when squeezed. That was from Donald. Poor Donald, she thought. He didn't even see her at her wonderful best. Kiera thought how beautiful the mermaid she had seen had looked and how now with all life gone, the vision was so cold.

The kettle whistled and Kiera retired to make two teas. Donald didn't usually take sugar, at least not at the wake. Still, she thought, he needs something to pick him up. Coming back into the bathroom, she found Donald now standing in the corner looking grimly at the deceased. His eyes were red from the tears and his face totally crestfallen.

"Where did you find her?" asked Kiera, passing him the tea.

"By the jetty, right down at the water. Face down. Turned her over. Tried mouth to mouth but nothing."

"Why up here then? I mean I don't mind that you did but why here? Surely there were a few houses a bit closer."

"Sunday. Bloody Sunday. I couldn't. Stood on someone's doorstep, breasts showing, tail there. I just thought. Well I thought you would know what to do. At least you wouldn't freak or be shocked."

"Okay Donald. I don't know what we'll do from here but okay."

"And I'm sorry."

"Sorry? Why?"

"For all this trouble, Kiera. Sorry. I mean interrupting you. At bath time too. Like every Sunday afternoon, your bath time."

"How do you know that?" Kiera shuffled nervously.

"You said. At the wake. Bath on a Sunday, shower every morning except the Sabbath. Lie in is what you said. I remember from the wake. We were chatting. Not for long but that's what you said. It was because of when your friend passed on. You never got your bath then. Oh, sorry. Shouldn't have brought that up."

Kiera was choking back some tears, memories of Marie's death still fresh. The pain of finding her friend that way. Peaceful but a shell of the life she had. As the image built up in her mind she erupted into a cry before burying her hands in her face and wailing loudly. Donald stepped across the room and held her tight. This time he felt the judders. He ignored the pain of some her tea spilling on his wrist and kept whispering it was okay.

After the moment had passed, she looked up into Donald's eyes. She saw he had been crying again. She saw his pain at her anguish, his plea to make it all go away being unanswered. That male desire to fix it all but finding all physical action to be impotent. And for that she was moved inside. Reaching up with her lips, she engulfed his mouth in a deep and prolonged kiss. Donald reciprocated and quickly took her tea from her hand lest she burned him again. Safety assured, he held her hips with both hands, felt her reach round to his backside and grip it tight. As the adrenalin pounded through him he started to slide his hands up her sides dragging the gown with him.

There was a sudden splash in the bath.

Kiera and Donald screamed together and held onto one

another lest they collapsed.

"She moved! Donald, she moved!"

Donald stared hard at the motionless mermaid in the bath. Her tail still seemed devoid of colour but her arms were developing a redness. The eyes were still closed but the gills at her neck seemed to move in the faintest of fashions.

"Kiera, she's not dead." Donald gripped Kiera's hands tight. "She's not dead, Kiera. Look, there's life there. Her gills, they're moving."

"Not that there's much chance of them being any use what with them being out of the water and that."

Donald raced over to the bath, grabbing the mermaid's hands, rubbing them like the insides would be gold. Kiera joined him, but in a more calculated fashion placed her hands at the neck and then the wrists.

"There's still no pulse, Donald. Nothing. It might just be body reacting to the heat."

"No, Kiera. Definitely not. Look! Kiera, just look at her chest. Damn, that's beautiful."

"Sorry?"

"It's rising and falling. Don't you see? She's breathing." The mermaid was starting to breathe and her nostrils were soon opening and closing ever so slightly as her body started to take pull in the necessary oxygen it required. Fascinated by this resurrection, Kiera could only stand, all reactions of her inner photographer silenced in wonder. Over the subsequent minutes, the mermaid started to show a flesh of deeper pink and the rise and the fall of her breathing deepened enough for Kiera to feel the need to cover the mermaid's exposed torso with a towel.

"The tail's changing colour too. Can you see that Kiera?

The sheens returning. I did it. She's coming back." Watching the smile leap across Donald's face, Kiera felt an enormous pride in the man she'd been holding just minutes before. His total disinterest in the mermaid's state of undress whilst acknowledging hers was also exciting her. She walked over to him and took his hand in hers. Together they watched the mermaid for a few brief moments before turning to each other, eyes glazed over. Resuming their previous embrace, they sought out each other, happy that their patient was now okay.

She screamed. Piercing their eardrums enough for the embrace to be broken, the mermaid was shrieking now and violently turning. White eyeballs with deep dark centers were wide open and the sharp teeth of her mouth were exposed.

"Donald, what the hell's up with her?"

"I don't know," said Donald clutching his ears. "She's my first mermaid."

"She must be in pain, surely. Gotta be a pain reaction."

"And on a Sunday. That noise is going to travel."

Donald tried grabbing the mermaid's arm but he was sent backwards as soon as he grabbed it. The strength of the creature stunned him and he reeled into the wall. Kiera jumped onto the Mermaid and was bounced about on top but managed to provide the loosest of restraints.

"Donald, she's boiling. She's so dammed hot. Look at her skin."

Reaching an arm round the mermaid, Kiera pulled the silver effect chain attached to the plug and the gurgle of disappearing water soon took over. Donald grabbed a moment of inspiration and turned on the cold tap before pushing down on the shower diverter. Cold water erupted from the head some five foot above covering Kiera and the mermaid. Gradually, the mermaid calmed down and Kiera looked at Donald as she tried to recover her breath. He was staring straight at her, soaking wet in her gown and exhausted from her recent exertions.

"I think you planned this," she said. Donald kept staring. "Donald! Clothes!"

"Right, of course." A blushing Donald raced out of the room. Wow, thought Kiera, bit of an interesting afternoon. She started to shiver and grabbed a towel to cover herself. Not that it matters now, he must have seen just about all there is to see. She looked down at the mermaid in the bath. It was true that the creature had calmed down but now it was watching Kiera intently. Occasionally it would look around briefly before settling back into monitoring Kiera. During one of these moments, it grabbed a fish shaped soap sitting at the end of the bath and bit down on it impatiently. A few seconds later, the mermaid spat out the soap and cupped water to its mouth. The scan for food began again.

Donald knocked on the door and came in on Kiera's request. She was about to criticise his choice of underwear but remembered these were the items that had been on her bed. They were the remnants of a hen weekend she had discovered in a shoebox that was cluttering up her bedroom. The shoebox was gone but she hadn't managed to get back to remove the offending items. It was amazing Donald was still standing given the lack of material involved in the item's manufacture.

Having not disillusioned Donald, she sent him to the living room while she dressed. Part of her felt for Donald's embarrassment in all this but in the other hand he had brought the problem to her. The mermaid was beautiful and Kiera watched her in wonder, similar to the day she had seen the blonde haired one at the beach.

There was a sudden belch from the mermaid but it looked unmoved by it. Hungry, Kiera reminded herself, she's hungry. She leaned out the door and called Donald.

"What do they eat, Donald?"

"I don't know," said Donald half squinting at Kiera at first, making sure this time she was decently dressed. This wasn't the sort of Sabbath he had been expecting. Certainly he couldn't remember any sermons that taught the proper actions for this sort of thing.

"She tried to eat a fish shaped soap of mine. Maybe fish, Donald. There's some fish in my fridge. Bit of salmon. Top shelf, can you get it?"

Donald duly returned with the salmon but asked Kiera should they not cook it. After asking if he was wise, Kiera proceeded to place the fish on the edge of the bath. After a few moments staring at it, the mermaid grabbed it greedily and stuffed it in to her mouth.

"Are there any more fish in the fridge, Donald?"

"I don't know. Didn't really look. Certainly never noticed anything."

"No matter, I'll take a look."

Kiera proceeded to her kitchen and scoured the fridge and the freezer in search of seafood. Having no luck in the fridge, all she found in the freezer was a bag of prawns. Emptying the packet into a bowl and then boiling a kettle, Kiera quickly defrosted them. Returning to the bathroom she placed the bowl on the bath edge in front of the mermaid. The creature just looked at the bowl. Ah, thought Kiera, and popped one into her mouth. The mermaid cautiously followed her lead before indulging herself in the shelled seafood.

Donald was now sitting on the chair in the corner of the bathroom, a little bedraggled and very worried looking. Crossing over to him, Kiera sat on his lap and placed her arms around him. He looked up at her face and she surprised him by giving him a long, deep kiss.

"Donald, you are a sweet, dear man. You're also one sexy beast but we have a problem. What do we do with her now you've brought her back to life?"

"Kiera, I don't know. I've no idea and I can't even go anywhere or do anything about it. Don't look so perplexed, it's the Sabbath. Nowhere's open." Kiera laughed heartily. "What's so funny?" asked Donald.

"Sunday, Donald. It's a Sunday and you've brought her back from the dead! Hope it's allowed."

# 6

# Murdo & Laura

The Reverend McKinney was having a bad Sabbath. The service this morning had gone reasonably well and he had even had an odd comment above "thank you for that" for a change but he was feeling quite forlorn. He had been here some seven years and was wondering what really had changed. Numbers in the flock had gone up but in honesty that was no measure of spiritual life. He would preach all year round on how to live this Christian life but to see some of the attitudes around him, his words may as well have been in Greek. And New Testament Greek at that.

Seminary hadn't built one up for the task of people but instead for ministry, whatever that was. According to some of his elders that was being a figurehead and an example to others, correcting their wrongs and condemning that blasted ferry. Everything was always so black and white to his more fervent elders. And usually their side was the white. Where was the contrition, the example of forgiveness to others? Behind it all, he was worried that, just maybe, the crux was being missed.

Donald in particular was bugging him. The young man

had started asking questions, mainly about the staunchly held views of his elders. In particular, the whole point and structure of church was causing Donald problems. Well at least someone was beginning to understand being a minister, thought Reverend McKinney.

The Reverend Murdo McKinney had married Laura Weston-Smith, some thirty years ago, down in deepest Somerset, just outside Taunton on a glorious summer's day. On that most blessed of days he had betrayed his roots, according to his mother, favouring Laura over Mairi who had grown up three crofts along from him. Mairi, in his mother's eyes, had been ideal. She was the daughter of the resident minister, extremely intelligent with a great command of the local language being a three time Mod winner. With her flowing black hair and slim tall figure, Mairi would have been quite a catch. She had made a play for him and Murdo had played along until that chance meeting.

It was Christmas Eve and he was assisting at a shelter in Bristol for the drunks and the down and outs. Standing behind a tray of bacon, which he was dispensing onto white rolls, he suddenly became breathless at the sight of her. A short but stout red headed woman, with a curvy figure and rotund face, was cleaning down a poor unfortunate who had just been sick as well as wetting himself. Showing no repugnance, she went about her task with cheer, constantly encouraging and sorting her client.

He had watched, entranced, until that heavily bearded man had angrily demanded "Where's my bloody bacon" in a loud voice. Laura had looked over and seen Murdo's embarrassment and beamed at him. After clear up that night, they had sat together over coffee until the small hours, talking about anything that came to mind, just wanting to remain in each other's company. Murdo was "burning" for her as the bible put it. And she burned too. It was a whirlwind six weeks he spent "down south" and his mother was disgusted when he returned home with a bride who was ten years older than him.

Laura had set him on fire and when he took up his first post on the mainland his mother cried, insisting he should come back to the island. His mother would be dead four years before he returned to a charge on the island. Ministers in these latter days were few and far between and so, even "wild" Murdo was voted back to his home with that "strange woman" in tow. He was sixty now and feeling older, his aches and pains somewhat more dominant. Laura at seventy was still a tour de force to be reckoned with and he thought she still had that ravishing spirit which had drawn him all those years ago.

He felt a hand tussle his fading hair. Laura extended a coffee in front of him before sitting in the chair opposite in front of the fire. The smell of burning peat always soothed him like the waft of freshly brewed coffee did.

"What's up, preacher man?"

Murdo looked up at Laura, the concern in her eyes evident, but soon reverted his eyes to the depths of his coffee.

"I said what's up? Don't think I won't tan your hide for being petulant, Murds."

"Sorry Westy. Just thinking."

"Donald again?" Murdo nodded.

"He'll be okay. You found your way. You questioned everything at one point. You got rid of the nonsense, kept the real stuff. Donald will too."

"Suppose he will. But he's right on so many things here.

Certainly got good points on other stuff. You know he brought us that coffee. It's fair trade. He made a point of that."

"And we buy fair trade too."

"Yes, but we don't. We, the church family don't. When we questioned it, all we got was, "we like the taste of the other, and we've always bought that one." How many points from the bible? I destroyed every sane argument but they just couldn't give a...."

"I'll not have you swearing in this house, no matter how much the subject deserves it."

"Sorry. But you understand. Of course you do. You always do."

"Have patience with people, Murds. He'll change them not you."

"But people like Donald will be pushed away."

"People like Donald will find their way because they are looking for the real thing. Trust God and have a bit of faith in Donald too. God sorted you. Besides Donald's smitten."

"He's ill?"

"To think you once had the fire burning inside. Oh, God grant me an ember." Laura smiled at Murdo to show her teasing. "He's in love, Murds."

"What, who?"

"Kiera. Didn't you see it?"

"When?"

"At the funeral. It's the same eyes a young man once flashed at me over a bacon roll."

"She's catholic. How's that going to work?"

"Probably better than a Presbyterian with an Anglican. We made it work, they will too."

Kiera, pondered Murdo. Certainly a giving heart, but also a

very free spirit. Not afraid to speak out or challenge a wrong. Donald would have his hands full. Murdo noticed Laura with her eyes focused on him.

"A man like Donald needs a free spirit like Kiera to push him to the greater things. A woman to believe in him, to challenge but ultimately stand beside him. And she needs that good soul to stand with, to lean on when the scaffolding collapses. Someone to believe in her."

"What makes you think that?"

"Because that's what you needed. And it's what I needed too."

Murdo laughed. Westy was always able to do that. Like a deep sea drill she would chip away into the core of him until she reached the rich oil beneath. It would flow to the surface and life would seem manageable again, at least for a little while. Rising from his chair, Murdo crossed to his wife and kissed her gently on the forehead.

"I'm not a baby, Murds. You can kiss me on the lips. Sometimes I think you're running for election with how you kiss me."

Laura got up and bent over to poke the fire. Feeling a sharp nip at her backside, she let go a giggle that defied her years.

"Don't start what you can't hope to finish young man," said Laura. This time there was a smack on her rear. Lord, I love him, she thought. Sitting back down, Laura awaited the return of her husband anticipating her Sunday afternoon hot chocolate. But then she heard the doorbell ring.

Sunday was truly a blessed day, as it was the one day when Murdo didn't get pestered for something silly from his kirk session. In fairness about fifty percent of them were normal, decent men who were genuinely doing their bit for the Lord with the best of intent. The rest ranged from being vacant to outright meanness.

There was quite a commotion at the door after she heard Murdo opening it. Voices were raised and excitable but Murdo's voice was absent. Then she heard the inner door close and her husband entered the living room again. Outside the hubbub continued.

"Westy, they have finally lost it."

"What's happened dear? What's got their knickers in a twist this time?"

"Mermaids, of all things, mermaids. Would you believe McKenzie has just asked me for the church's position on mermaids? Free will, predestination, original sin, heaven and hell and forgiveness, these I can deal with. But, tell me, when did I take the seminary course on mermaids? Was it an option I passed up? Mermaids." Reverend McKinney looked deep into his fire and sadly shook his head.

"What's started all of this then? Have they been at the drink over lunch?"

"No. Sad to say they are as sober as judges. It's the boat, or the ship of evil as MacLeod calls it. They reckon someone has shot some film of mermaids off the back of it."

Laura raised an eyebrow. "Filmed it. It's a hoax, no doubt, sent to wind up or promote passenger figures for the summer."

"Laura, they say there's proof. It's on that internet thing you get those sermons on."

"YouTube?"

"Yes, that one. Apparently it's full resolution. McKenzie says it's a scandal but it's true. He's seen it."

"Sunday surfing, eh? I thought he was against the television on Sundays."

"What do I tell them, Laura? I have just about had enough of all this shenanigans."

"Calm down Murds and keep them outside 'til I get a look at the post."

Laura reached under the magazine on the occasional table and placed her tablet on her lap. Typing mermaids and the name of the port into the search engine soon brought a response. Selecting the video section highlighted several posts with the ferry displayed in the pictures. Selecting the topmost one, Laura grabbed Murds close and together they watched.

A smiling child was seen waving at the camera. By the rolling horizon in the background, it was clear that the sea was in a rough state and that many people had ventured outside in the hope that the air might somehow stabilise their stomachs. Then there was a shout and the camera spun round to the sea. There was a figure in the distance but the gap between the ferry and this wave surfer was too far to identify with the camera's particular resolution. Over the next minute, several more dots appeared and they began making ground on the ferry. As the figures appeared and then submerged, the people on the deck began to gather at the safety railings, desperate for a better view.

About two minutes into the film, a figure emerged approximately twenty feet from the ferry. It appeared to be a blonde woman, torso above the waterline and in a state of undress. Over the next three minutes, such women but with varying hair colour would appear and then disappear beneath the waves. As each dived to the depths a tail could be seen flicking upwards behind them before following them down.

"That has to be a fake, Laura. Some sort of wind up."

"Darling, look at the people there. Don't you recognise some of them? There's quite a few I know. If this is a fake it is incredibly well done. Murds, I think this might just be for real."

Murdo stood in silence staring at the screen. The wall clock chimed five o'clock but he never flinched. Laura continued to watch the different up-loadings. Outside, Reverend McKinney's session were continuing their restlessness and began to knock the door again.

"Laura, dear, would you kindly put the tablet away and I will bring the mob inside?"

"I doubt they'll mind the tablet."

"Laura, let's not wake the lion today, thank you." Her wife tutted but consented to her husband's request. After a few minutes, the twelve strong party of enraged churchmen had gathered into the living room.

"It's a disgrace Reverend, something needs to be done about it."

"Well Iain, what would you have me do?" Murdo looked at his oldest elder, feigning interest in his response.

"As I see it they need to be banned. Keep them away from the ferry and our shores. We need to put pressure on the council to take action against them. It's the devil's work to be sure."

"Yes," agreed Angus MacIver, session clerk, "clearly they are from the devil."

"The devil's becoming quite artistic with his minions," interjected Laura and received a dour look from her husband.

"The devil's work indeed," echoed Iain Macleod the original elder, in a dismissive gesture to the only lady in the room.

"Why the devil?" pondered the Reverend.

"Well, they are unnatural. There ain't no mermaids in the

bible."

"Well," sighed Murdo, "there aren't any gnus either."

"True Minister, true but these mermaids, well, they could be violent! There's always been tales of these creatures in the sea, luring sailors."

"Thank you Iain but there's also here there be dragons and the edge of the world to worry about too."

"Yes, Reverend McKinney, but these mermaids, do you see how they look? They are corrupted and on the Sabbath day too."

"Iain, I am struggling to follow you on this one. What's your point?"

"Well minister, they are.......exposed!"

"Yes," agreed Angus, "exposed!"

"I agree it would be cold for them but surely being in the depths of the sea they would be used to the temperature."

"No, minister, it is not their welfare I seek to assist, rather their mode of dress."

"Well, they don't have any clothes Iain."

"Exactly. They are exposed. And on a Sunday too. You see the devil's work."

"So Iain, as I understand it, you are affronted at the exposed mammary glands of sea dwelling creatures being exposed, particularly on this day of the week."

"Indeed. I believe the Reverend McAlpine is going to protest about these exposed breasts, provided by the devil to titillate our young men. Have you seen the depravity of it, arousing young men's minds to the sexual impulse? Soon we shall have all sorts of debauchery here, if this is allowed unchecked."

Murdo heard his wife snicker and struggled to suppress a laugh himself. The arrival of the mermaids was quite shocking but the attitude taken by his session, or rather by Iain, was less surprising. Father, he thought, give me some wisdom on this.

"Well minister, what are you going to do?"

"I will pray Iain."

"Pray, is that it minister, just pray. I think some action needs to be taken."

"Maybe so. May God guide me, Iain. Now, I have a service to be thinking about and I look forward to seeing you all tonight. If in the meantime you feel that the sight of these creatures is too much, I suggest you avert your eyes and show our young men an example. I shall see you later all, thank you so much for bringing this to my attention."

With practiced ease, Laura ushered the men to the door and closed it behind her. Returning to the room she saw her husband in thoughtful pose in his chair.

"Well done Murdo. Avert your eyes. Maybe we can hold a sale of works in order to raise some money for a few bikinis or swimsuits." Murdo didn't rise to the bait.

"Poor creatures, Laura. They should have stopped in the deep. Now we'll see the wicked ways of our world, mark my words. Now they have something to exploit."

"All God's creatures Murdo, all God's creatures." The Reverend McKinney smiled.

# 7

# You can Lead a Horse...

All was quiet in the bathroom. They had left the door half open but had decided to give the mermaid some quiet after the excitement of the day. Donald, sat in an easy chair watching the door, was becoming worried. It was now eleven o'clock at night and he had missed the evening service. Given the situation, Donald wasn't going to leave Kiera in the lurch but he knew he would have to have his excuses ready. This was a problem as there weren't many solutions presenting themselves for consideration.

The Reverend McKinney was always saying that you should tell the truth but surely this was the exception to the rule. There was the problem of the mermaid but at least that had just occurred. There was nothing he could have done about that and he did reach out to help. No, it was the issue of explaining why he had been at Kiera's. Not only that but in her bathroom and then seeing her in her bath albeit with a gown on. Not that it had stopped him seeing everything. And on a Sunday too.

Inside he had a warm glow, generated by Kiera's reaction to him. For the last three months he had looked forward to any chance he had of seeing her and had played out how he would gradually get closer to her. Bit by bit and with the deepest of propriety, he would engage her in conversation before stunning her with an elaborate meal and a first kiss along the sea shore. Bursting into her house carrying a topless fish girl while Kiera was scantily clad was not a plan he had thought of. While he was nervous of the consequences, part of Donald was deeply excited by this turn of events.

Kiera came through from her bedroom, dressed in warm pyjamas with a broad grin on her face. She hadn't seen it coming but looking back she could remember how Donald had been "about" these last few months. Always on the edge of the conversation, she now remembered his ever cheery face whenever she caught his eye. Inside she was quivering, which was a new sensation, as she prided herself on being able to stand alone in everything. Donald was shaking that desire to the core and more surprisingly, she was delighted with this turn of events.

"Donald, did you ring your Mum?"

"Yes. I said you had had some urgent problems with the house and I was sorting them. The gas cylinders if anyone asks. And I'm going night fishing so they won't look for me until tomorrow."

"Good."

"I don't like lying to her."

"I'm not sure she could handle the truth at the moment." Kiera popped her head into the bathroom before walking over to Donald and sitting down on his lap. Throwing her arms around him, she gave him another long, deep kiss.

"Now that's enjoyable. You're a dark horse, Donald. It's okay, you can hold me tight. In fact, it would be better if you did."

Awkwardly at first, Donald wrapped his arms around Kiera, careful to not touch an area by accident he thought may still be out of bounds. Kiera hadn't complained at anything he had done, and although he was itching to come closer physically, part of him was worried of doing something wrong, scaring her off.

"So you have your cover story, what excitement are you going to show me tonight?" Donald looked shocked at what Kiera was implying. "No," laughed Kiera, "what are we going to do about my house guest?" A little sigh of relief came from Donald and he relaxed.

"How about we wait until the wee hours and then I could take her down to the shore. Maybe wade out with her into the water and she can disappear off back to wherever she normally swims."

"Okay but is she fit enough for that?"

"I don't know. What do we do? Call a vet?"

"I get you Donald, sure we'll do that. About two or three a.m. then. We can't keep her for long in here anyway. Might as well get comfortable fella as we have a wee wait on our hands." Kiera rose up and wandered over to the radio. Switching it on, she strode over to the lights and knocked them off. In the dim light Donald watched her clamber back onto him and shove down tight.

The music of the station was varied and between gently exchanged kisses, the two rather tired friends hung on tight. Occasional splashes were heard from the bathroom but an air of peace reigned in the house as the midnight hour approached. Kiera was half-dozing as the news came on when midnight was struck.

"Reports are coming in of a shoal of mermaids being sighted off a ferry servicing the Scottish islands. The Loch Balerna was carrying out its normal Sunday afternoon crossing when several mermaids were seen in the water close to the ship's wake......."

The new lovers sat motionless as the report described how several video clips of the incident had gone viral around the world with many experts stating this was no hoax. Mermaid societies and hunters were now converging on the ferry route along with the world's media. There was then a tirade against these creatures of the devil, brandishing their nakedness on the Sabbath by one of the stricter Island ministers.

"Do you get the feeling we need to get her back offshore tonight Donald?" Donald just nodded. Kiera stood up and disappeared into her bedroom before returning with an alarm clock. Manipulating the rear to set the clock, she then placed it on the table bedside Donald.

"Two hours shut eye and then we go. Where do you wanna sleep?" Donald blushed heavily. "The chair or the bed?" Donald went totally red. "Donald, I'm not being forward. You take one and I'll take the other." Inside Donald was in turmoil. Half of him wanted Kiera to be forward but the rest of him felt apprehensive.

"Why not the chair for both of us?" Kiera smiled and settled into Donald's arms. Although excited, the events of the day were taking a toll on Donald and he soon fell asleep. Kiera looked at his face with eyes closed and took a moment to appreciate a day when a lot of things were changing. Slowly, she drifted off to sleep as well.

There was a loud ringing beside his head. Instinctively

Donald stood up pitching Kiera onto the floor. Quickly his senses came back to him and he reached down to pick her back up. A mumbled sorry was accepted and Kiera popped her head into the bathroom to check on her house guest.

The mermaid was slumbering too and was quite motionless. Good thought Kiera. Telling Donald to gently wake up their guest, Kiera retired to the bedroom to change. Returning in a black t-shirt and leggings, she noticed and appreciated Donald's survey of her before grabbing a fleece jacket.

"You'll have to carry her, Donald. She would be too heavy for me and I think one on the arms and one on the tail is not going to be very practical."

"We may also rip her arms off." Kiera smiled. His humour was very dry.

Kiera entered the bathroom and spoke soothingly to the mermaid. She stroked her long hair and brought Donald down to his knees to sit close by the bath. Although pretty sure the mermaid couldn't understand her language, she tried by signs and actions to indicate their present intentions. Soon Donald was picking up the mermaid and carrying her in his arms. Kiera watched with just a hint of jealousy as her new man crossed the house with a bare chested woman. It was a good job she stank of fish.

Kiera switched off the lights in the house and opened the door gently. At this hour of the night the landscape was totally dark, the street lights having been switched off around midnight. Walking ahead, Kiera gently trod over the uneven ground checking for large rocks that often were half-submerged into the underlying peat. Taking a direct line to the sea, the trio walked through the middle of some disinterested sheep left at peace in their croft.

This particular night was cool but calm with half the sky covered with an indistinct layer of cumulus cloud. The air upwind of the mermaid was fresh and soon the sea breeze was pushing Kiera's hair back from her face, allowing her skin to embrace this refreshing wind.

After a while she heard a forced whisper behind her.

"Kiera. Kiera, wait." She turned and saw Donald a good hundred meters behind, face dripping with sweat. She had become lost in the place and had forgotten to keep the pace reasonable.

"Keep going Donald," she encouraged, "there's not much left to go now. I can see the jetty."

"No, don't. Keep to the left. Can you see the jutting rock over on the left? Keep left of that. It's an easy path down to the shore, albeit rocky, and we shouldn't run into any night fishermen."

Kiera nodded and a little shiver ran down her back. Up until now she hadn't even entertained the idea that someone might catch them. It was two in the morning. Who in their right mind would be prancing about except mermaid protecting lunatics? The danger of the situation became very clear to her. The threat in that minister's voice on the radio made her start to shake just a little.

It took another ten minutes before they reached the rocky shoreline. Donald, mermaid in arms, clambered down to the edge of the water. He stepped out up to his knees in the sea, before setting the mermaid into the water. She dropped under the surface and Donald made his way back to stand beside Kiera on the shore.

He felt cold and he dripped from his knees down. Kiera grabbed hold of him and hugged him tight.

"She's free, Donald. You saved her. She's clear to go back to wherever. Away from any trouble. Well done you." Kiera turned Donald's head and reached up to kiss him. For a few moments they enjoyed one another before curiosity drove them to stare out to sea, hoping to grab a last view of their visitor. There was nothing to see. Just a gently rippling tide.

Kiera took Donald's hand and they turned away from the shore to start their climb back up the crofts. With the mermaid gone, her mood lost its nervous edge and she looked forward to some quiet hours, cuddled in the arms of her Donald. He too was breathing easier after his exertions and his step seemed to be lighter. Kiera was going to enjoy these hours before sunrise. Now was a time to chat and tease and kiss.

They heard a splash. Then something breaking out of the water. Then that seal-like call. Donald turned first, running back to the sea. The mermaid was in the same spot they had left her with a sorrowful look in her eyes. He splashed his way up to her and then just stopped dead. How do you ask what's wrong, he thought? He turned and saw Kiera at the rock edge.

"Kiera, I don't know what's wrong. She's just sitting upright. There's no movement."

"Try to show her Donald. Ask if she can swish her tail?"

"I don't speak mermaid."

"No, you don't need to. Just use your hands, your body, whatever."

He's trying, thought Kiera, but God bless him, he's making an arse of it. Kiera stepped down into the water beside Donald and started making hand signals at the mermaid. After a while of making figures in the air and receiving them back, Kiera felt she knew what was wrong.

"Donald there's something wrong with her tail. It seems

like she can't move it very far. Poor thing can't swim."

"What are we going to do? She was meant to swim off. Should I take her further out, do you think that will help?"

"No, Donald. She can't swim. We need to get her looked at. We'll have to take her back." Donald swore. "Sorry, but we can't leave her here. If they find her she'll be all over the news and that. She'll be a freak for them. Sorry Donald, but you'll need to carry her back to mine."

Kiera tried to sign their intent and believed the mermaid had understood. Only then did she let Donald approach the creature and once again pick her up to carry. He looks so tired thought Kiera, poor guy's shattered.

It was a long, slow trudge back up the crofts to the house. As it was still dark, Kiera once again led the way pointing out jutting rocks and this time taking care to stay within reasonable distance. Occasionally they stopped as Kiera thought she saw movement but then realising the trick of the night she encouraged them on.

On entering the house, Donald placed the mermaid back in the bath and turned on the cold tap. Returning to the lounge, he found Kiera changed back into her pyjamas. In one hand she had a steaming cup of tea which he took gratefully.

"You need to get out of those wet things Donald or you'll catch your death of cold."

"Have you got something for me to change into?"

"No worries Donald, I'll get the duvet for you, you can wrap yourself in that. Get stripped and I'll put your clothes through the wash." As Kiera left the room, Donald self-consciously removed his clothes and stood naked in the middle of the room. A single hand covered his modesty when she returned and she teased him by giving a good up-and-down stare before handing him the duvet. His embarrassment was obvious.

"Sorry, that was cruel. But I liked what I saw."

Donald hugged the duvet tight as he sat in the chair. He watched Kiera enter the bathroom, heard the tap being switched off and then she emerged and stood before him. Donald froze in his seat and Kiera let out a brief tut of annoyance before sweeping back the duvet and sitting on Donald's lap. The duvet was then quickly pulled back over them again.

"Donald, relax. You've made it, just enjoy these feelings. I know I am." Donald was exhausted and his previous experience with women was not extensive. He found Kiera putting him on a wondrous edge and her forwardness was a shock after longing for her with no real belief that he would ever have a chance. He slipped his arms around her and buried his face into her hair. He breathed deeply trying to take in her essence. "Kiera."

"Yes, Donald."

"Don't take this the wrong way but.....you smell of fish."

Kiera laughed. "I think we both do. But if you are edging for a tandem bath, I'm afraid the tub's already taken. We'll get a wash in the morning. You can scrub me down." She giggled at the shock crossing his face.

# 8

# Down the Town

Laura McKinney struggled to park the car due to the large amounts of traffic in town that Saturday. Since the discovery of the mermaids almost a week ago there had been an influx of the nation's media, all seeking to be the first to capture these exciting creatures on camera. Inclement weather had prevented the ferry from sailing from Monday to Thursday and had meant that the anticipated explosion of interest in the mermaids had been a relative damp squib. Nothing had been seen and most of the equipment and broadcasting vans had been stuck on the mainland. Local news had only been able to report on bleak weather and the power cuts suffered had dominated headlines.

Saturday was a fine weather day and with most of the media having arrived on the Friday sailings, the media circus was beginning to take hold. Many experts had taken center stage, detailing how these creatures could be living out at sea, away from the sight of man. Speculation raged about how many existed and if there was a male of the species. Various mermaid appreciation groups and "believers" also arrived to join in the fun.

Having eventually found a car park space a little way from the town centre, Laura defied her years by marching smartly into the hubbub. She was looking for a new duvet as the old one had started spitting feathers and with the only local outlet being located in town, she had little option on this busy day other than to risk all the noise and excitement. She could have ordered online of course but she was a true believer in the shop local idea and despite the lack of customer service she often endured, she continued to spend Murdo's money in the town he grew up with.

There was something of a carnival atmosphere as off-island opportunists had arrived brandishing mermaid balloons and trinkets, hiking up and down the sea front, calling out their wares. A reporter from a television channel tried to accost Laura for an interview but she politely declined and continued amid the dizzying array of people. She nodded to various local people she knew and watched them gawking.

Then she drew upon a curious sight. One mainland paper had arrived with its topless models, famous for showing significant frontage. They were sitting on the sea wall with fake fish tails on their legs and bikini tops. The five girls, side by side, were being shouted at by various ministers with several members of their congregations. A photographer was imploring the church folk to move as they were blocking the light for his shoot. The girls were being labelled as anything from harlots to the spawn of the devil for their actions. Trying to pose but obviously affected by these calls, the girls would retort, occasionally using the odd obscenity.

Laura tried to ignore the whole thing and pass by. Being a minister's wife, there was no easy way out of any argument that she engaged in. As nonchalant as she was, skirting round the incident, Laura was clocked by Mrs McAllan, wife of the Reverend McAllan, always staunch whatever the issue.

"Mrs McKinney, come here Laura. Laura, come here and see this. Isn't it disgusting, Laura, right here on our wee island?" Laura sent a silent request to her Jesus to be with her and turned into the middle of the crowd.

"Mrs McAllan, so good to see you, now what exactly is all this furore about?"

"Well, Mrs McKinney, would you believe it? This man here, a photographer, wants to take pictures of these young girls in a state of undress. And all because of those heathen mermaids. The devil's at work in this. Polluting God's own wee island with this sort of filth. They should be disgusted at themselves, exposing their bosoms like that. And as for him," she pointed at the photographer, "it's no wonder we get rapists and perverts nowadays. Get back to the mainland with you all, get back I say."

With the tirade complete, Mrs McAllan started into a rendition of the 23rd Psalm, vigorously joined by the little group of church women around her. Laura thought for a moment and then took the photographer to one side.

"I'm sorry my good man, my name's Laura, just a concerned resident. I was wondering exactly, what you are going to do here?" The photographer looked a little taken aback at Laura's relaxed attitude but responded pleasantly enough.

"Hi, I'm Gerald, photographer working for the nationals. Basically I'm trying to get a picture of the girls here at the sea wall, looking like mermaids. Tie in with all this fuss about the real ones. It's a good link for us what with the mermaids showing their boobs all the time, bit like our models."

"So what, you're going to shoot the girls topless here at the wall. Right now, in the middle of town, in the middle of the day."

"Bloody hell, no. I told that other woman, all we are doing is bikini shots with fish tails on. We can't just go popping the boobs out in the town willy-nilly. Cops would do us right away. And here I'd probably get lynched."

"Yes, you probably would." Laura thought for a moment. "Do you mind if I have a word with the girls?"

"Knock yourself out. It's not like I can get anything done with these clowns jumping into my light."

"Thank you." Laura turned to the girls sat on the wall.

"Hi there, my name's Laura. I have to say you girls look absolutely stunning. God certainly blessed you with looks. I just wanted to say welcome to the island and sorry about all this fuss."

"Fuss is right," declared the buxom red head closest to Laura, "I'm used to us causing a stir and even some jealously but that woman called me a harlot and then the spawn of Satan."

"Yeah," said the brunette in the middle of the group, "What's up with her? Right bloody prude. Ain't she ever been proud of her boobs. They're all natural here."

"I don't doubt," said Laura, "but you need to understand this place. I'm not saying they are right but they do have their reasons. Tell you what, why don't you come up to mine for some drinks at some point. In fact the sooner the better. We can have a right good natter. Here's the address. Are you free this afternoon?"

The brunette girl walked over to her photographer who after a brief conversation seemed to give his consent. Returning to Laura, the girl agreed they would come up at about two o'clock as they were going to do some night shots now when they could get a bit more privacy. Behind her Laura heard the disgruntled voice of Mrs McAllan in shocked disbelief bemoaning Laura's interactions with the model group. Nothing new there, she thought.

Laura crossed the road and headed to the local book store hoping to pick up the latest thriller. Continuing her support for local traders, she shunned the online stores when possible but often certain items were unavailable. More often "modern concepts" such as fair-trade and animal welfare foodstuffs were not always embraced and she found her principals challenged. Nonetheless she persisted.

Glancing at the window display of the book store, Laura saw an abundance of books dedicated to mermaids. From young readers to anything remotely adult related. In fact, hidden away towards the back was something described as "an erotic adventure for the modern woman". She laughed at the sultry idea of the mermaid, contrasting with their seemingly fish-like tendencies.

Inside, she saw young Iain McClaren. The poor lad had never really gotten over the death of his father and that uncle of his didn't help. He always seemed such a loner, bit of a lost soul. Apparently, he was dipping into the fishing books today. Oh well, thought Laura, let's see how he is today.

"Hi Iain, how's you?"

"Quite busy, Mrs McKinney."

"Oh, aye. And what with, may I ask?"

"Well now that I have been proven right about my Dad, I think I should get some justice."

"Okay, Iain. So you think the footage is definitely real? There's a lot of debate."

"I know what I saw, even back then as a child I saw them.

They're not the pretty little things everyone makes them out to be. They're killers. Murders. And I'm gonna catch one and prove it."

"How you going to do that? No one's caught one. There's going to be lots of people looking for them."

"I will. That's what I'm looking up. Just mind, Mrs McKinney, they are evil things. Take care if you see one."

"I will Iain, I will. God bless."

Laura edged away worried by Iain's fixation. The boy was definitely unhinged, and who could blame him suffering that trauma at such an early age. Part of Laura hoped it was all a hoax. She hoped for the sake of Iain and for many of the islanders it would all go away and life could settle down again. Then she wondered was this such a good thing. Surely this shake-up might make people think. Maybe the ingrained ideas or indoctrinated thoughts could be broken. Still, she should hurry up as she had to pick something up for these girls arriving at the house that afternoon. It would be good to have a chat with them but no doubt Murdo would give her one of his wry looks. The poor man would get it in the neck from his session. It would bother him but he would back her as it was the right thing to do.

He had laughed when she gave him that little plastic wristband. WWJD. What Would Jesus Do. "Now you're asking" he had said. But she had seen him glancing at it at times, reflecting on it. And he did do it. Generally. He certainly tried, which given his roots in the place was quite something. Loving a place was hard, thought Laura. It's just like loving a child. They have your love no matter what. Just because they are a part of you. But you have to stand up to things they do wrong. You have to show them what is right. Set the example.

And then, just sometimes, they get it. Then they call you all the names of the day, say they don't want you and sometimes plain ignore you. But you love them still. She got that Murdo loved this place but she found that love so desperately hard to match.

Time was moving on and Laura still had a few extras to pick up from the drop-in convenience store, so she walked briskly shouting a few "hellos" as she passed by some of Murdo's flock. Eggs were needed and now that she had these girls popping up, she would need a few cakes and biscuits. Maybe some drinks too. Wine was the thing nowadays, very sociable afternoon drink. Oh well, she'd get one of those boxes which kept for months then it wouldn't go to waste.

Laura was used to shopping at the larger version on the edge of town and didn't come into this particular store often. The eggs had decided to hide themselves amongst the tight isles and she circled the store three times before seeing the black hair of a girl she had been thinking about. With the freezer door open, Kiera was staring at the fish section. After a moment she removed every packet of plain frozen fish into her basket. Laura watched astounded at the quantities Kiera was taking. Kiera tried a furtive look around her but only succeeded in catching Laura's eye.

"Kiera, child, how are you?"

"Fine, just fine Laura."

"What's with all the fish? Some sort of Irish festival or something? Or is it for one of your pictures."

"Oh...... yes, that's it, Laura. Pictures....... a grand composition I'm doing."

"Excellent dear. Most be costing you a fortune though. If there's any fish left over in good condition I'll take them off your hands for you. Help you with the cost."

"The cost?"

"Yes, dear. Of the fish."

"Oh...... okay, yes. Thanks. Thank you."

"Are you alright?"

"Just been a little under the weather."

"Oh that's right. Donald's mum said. Said he was taking stuff round to you, looking after you. Nice young man, Donald. Got an eye for you I reckon, Kiera." Kiera's pale skin blushed and she turned her eyes to the floor. "Anyhow, good luck with the photo."

"What photo?"

"The one of all these fish."

"Oh ..... Yes, thanks." Kiera turned to away. She's awfully distracted, thought Laura, wonder if she's alright. I know. She can help me today and I'll see just how good she is.

"Kiera. Kiera dear, just a minute."

"Wah, what is it?"

"Kiera, have a favour to ask. I have some models coming up to the house for afternoon tea....... or maybe wine actually, but I need some company. I can't get any of the church ladies as the girls are those topless models from the paper. Need someone normal to talk to them. Would you come round? With your figure you'll not be out of place. Gorgeous girl like yourself."

"You're a flatterer, Laura. But a good one at it. Okay I shall try. About two, if that's okay." Laura nodded. "I just need to check what Donald's doing."

"Oh aye, didn't realise he gotten that interested." Kiera was embarrassed but underneath a beaming smile came through.

"He's very sweet, Laura. He's great in fact."

"Happy for you, dear. Two o'clock and I want details sometime soon." Kiera smiled but there was a worry on her face. Laura let her go, rather than ask any more questions. She'll tell me if she wants to.

It took Laura another five minutes to pick up the rest of her items. There was a young lad on the till, maybe sixteen, she reckoned. They got so tall these days but he still had the spotty complexion of an adolescent. And he's watching me quite intently.

"Ten forty nine please."

"There you go. Busy in town today."

"Yes. And one change........ Can I ask something?" The youth looked concerned.

"Certainly."

"The woman with the black hair you were speaking to."

"Yes, my friend. What about her?"

"Well, I was wondering. She has been in her every day this week buying up all our salt and fish. Does she keep some sort of animals? It's just all a bit weird."

Blimey thought Laura. What possible purpose could she have? What weird thing were Kiera and Donald into? I never thought that either of them were the kinky type. Then something clicked in Laura's mind.

"People are weird, young man. As a shop assistant, it's best not to be so pass remarkable. Have a good day."

# 9

# A Ministerial Visit

Murdo McKinney, having buried one of his less faithful flock, had found himself with time on his hands. There was probably another hour or so before Laura would be getting home and making lunch so he decided to pay a visit to someone with whom his wife had an enjoyable familiarity. Once, Murdo had owned a camera and had taken, what he described as, good amateur shots. When he had arrived on the island, he came across a little studio, located in the garage of a brunette Irish girl. Her candour was lively and challenging and her pictures showed her to be a kindred spirit in the art world.

Being forward, Laura had encouraged their meeting to discuss photography and general difficulties with settling in on the island. His session had visited him on more than one occasion about the inappropriateness of visiting a Catholic and such a young and vibrant woman. Their actual words had been attractive and frisky. Murdo chuckled to himself. Kiera was fun and certainly challenging of his dog collar but to believe he was being dragged into an affair was laughable. What did they think of Laura, as she encouraged him in his friendship? Probably best not to ask what they thought of Laura.

Kiera had a keen eye for a shot and her pictures took Murdo back to his early days with Laura, when she would appear in shy fashion in his pictures. A friend Kiera certainly was, but also a prompt not to abandon those wonderful days of promise when he had started out on this path for his Lord.

Having been told Kiera had been unwell all week and rarely seen out of the house, Murdo decided he should pop along and see if he could render any help. Stopping the car at the end of the short drive, he strode up to the door and went to knock before halting, realising he hadn't brought anything for the ill. Oh well, I'm here now, so I'll have to be the balm.

Three loud knocks of his hand on the door rang out across the crofts before Murdo remembered the bell. Stepping back, he noticed all the curtains were closed and there was a definite air of a fortress about the house. Oh well, he thought, better have a look and see if she's in. Murdo strode down to the edge of the house hoping to see in the display room window before he heard a call behind him.

"Reverend McKinney. Can I help you?"

"Ah, Donald my boy. How are you? Would Kiera be in at all, I heard she wasn't well."

"Well she's okay now, Reverend McKinney." I can't lie to a minister, thought Donald.

"Good Donald, that is good. I was going to have a wee cuppa with her if she was up to it."

"Well, Minister, she's not here."

"Donald, stop this minister nonsense. My name is Murdo and you can use that well and proper. Where is Kiera then?"

"She went out shopping. I think she needed to stock up after being ill."

"So she was here when you got here?"

"Yes," said Donald. Strictly, this was correct. On arriving with the mermaid at the beginning of last week Kiera had been here. The fact that Donald had been here all week and not, as his Mum had been informed "obsessed with the night fishing", was something he wanted to remain quiet. Despite having slept on the sofa each night, Donald wasn't sure the Reverend McKinney would approve. And he certainly wasn't going to tell him Kiera was prone to joining him in her pyjamas with a large duvet in the middle of the night.

"When will she be back?"

"Hopefully soon. She's bringing back some lunch."

"Excellent, I'll come in and wait."

"No! You can't, minister."

"Why not? And it's Murdo." Ah, pondered Donald, why not? I can hardly say there's a semi-naked mermaid in the bath. Think, Donald, think.

"Ah well, you see, it's just that ........... well ......... it's not that ...... but ...., yes, it's the state of the place. She's been unwell and well there's a kinda smell about the place. Bit fusty with all the illness and that. Sickly smell, so she wouldn't want to, be a bit embarrassed. You understand."

"Donald, it's me. I visit hospitals all the time. It's no problem, let me in and I'll sit down and wait."

Donald found himself forced back and Reverend McKinney strode into the room and sat down on the comfiest armchair. We sat there cuddling this morning, thought Donald. And a bit more. Gotta get him out of here quick.

"Rever ... Murdo, I'm sure she'll be back soon. She'll pop over if you want I'm sure."

"Nonsense, Donald. I'm fine just here." There was a splash from the bath.

"Did I hear something?"

"Nothing, no. I heard nothing."

"I did, Donald, like a splash, water of some sort. I'm sure I heard something." Another splash. "There it is again. Where's that coming from?"

"Must be the washing machine, I think it's on heavy rinse cycle of something. She's probably got muddy shoes in it or something."

"Why would she have muddy shoes? Donald, the girl hasn't been out, she's been unwell."

"I know but maybe she hadn't got round to doing them until now. That'll be it, definitely. Been unwell and then catching up with the washing."

"What brought you over, Donald?" Donald's eyes went into a panic. He hadn't been expecting that question.

"Well, I was just looking to help. See if Kiera was okay."

"Okay and she left you here." Not going well, thought Donald.

"Yes, she needed shopping. I said I would try and do some tidying up for her." Beside the chair the Reverend McKinney was occupying, a black object grabbed Donald's view. His heart sunk and part of him started to shake. A black bra of Kiera's was lying next to the chair, soo close that Donald was amazed the minister hadn't seen it already. Then again, maybe he had. Maybe that was where the questions had come from. There was another splash from the bathroom.

"What's that noise Donald? Surely it's not the washing machine. Something might be broken or a tap running in the bathroom. Shall I go check?"

"No! No, no ....... it's fine. I'll have a look. Why don't you pop out into the kitchen?"

"The kitchen?"

"Yes. Cup of tea. Pop the kettle on. I'll see what's the issue with that sound."

"Okay Donald. As you wish, I don't know where anything is, but okay. Do you take milk?"

"Everything," said Donald. Murdo got up and walked into the kitchen shaking his head. Grabbing the bra, Donald quickly opened the bathroom door where he saw the mermaid desperately trying to reach a fish that had fallen onto the floor. He tossed it back into the bath and shut the door behind him. Turning round he met Murdo face to face.

"Was just wondering where the tea bags are? Oh, that a bra in your hand?"

"Yes. One of Kiera's." The obviousness of the statement struck Donald.

"One would imagine. Hard to tell with lingerie so I prefer to let it all stay a secret. Not sure I would be able to pick out Laura's."

"Well this one is definitely Kiera's. She doesn't like it particularly, as it unsnaps at the front. She's always making a grab at the back like her other bras before she remembers." Donald froze. Murdo stared at the floor and made a slight cough.

"The tea bags. Whereabouts in the kitchen?"

"On the left. Second shelf in the cupboard."

"Right. I'll get it. Why don't you tidy Kiera's things away? Probably best we don't find any more remnants lying around." Donald nodded. Blast, he thought. Kiera's going to freak. I sounded like some mad sort of voyeur. He either thinks I'm living in sin with her or I'm a raging pervert looking in her windows. Donald heard the crunch of footsteps on the path.

The door swung open and Kiera seeing Donald smiled broadly.

"Hi there, Tiger. What a morning, I could do with sexy cuddle." Donald's face lit up like slow down speed boards on the roads. Kiera couldn't put the brakes on and weighed down by bags of fish and salt she crossed the room and kissed him deeply. Donald stood still like a statue.

"What's up? Hands been cut off. They weren't so shy this morning."

"Good afternoon Kiera, I'm just making a cuppa, would you like one?" Kiera nearly fainted. Her normally pale cheeks went a deep red. She looked quizzically at Donald who just shook his shoulders saying what could I do? Time to act normal, thought Kiera.

"Ah, Murdo, good to see you. How are you? Cuppa would be great."

"I'm fine Kiera but how are you, yourself. Not been well I am told."

"Just woman's things," said Kiera, using the code words that all men naturally shy away from.

"Oh, right. But okay now then."

"Yes, thanks for asking. And for visiting, good of you. I haven't many pictures for you to see as I haven't been out, Murdo. Still maybe soon with this decent weather arriving."

"Aye, I wasn't looking for any pictures but just checking you were okay."

"I met Laura in town actually. She's invited me across in an hour or so." Donald's face this time looked quizzical.

"Excellent, I can walk you over, Kiera. In fact, come over as well Donald." Flicking his eyes to Kiera, indicating the direction of the bathroom, Donald stayed quiet.

"What's up Donald, lost your tongue?" Kiera shook her

shoulders and Donald reluctantly answered in the affirmative. For the next half hour, the young couple listened to Murdo describing the madness over the town regarding these mermaids. He was of the opinion it was probably all a hoax or some sort of social experiment by one of the larger universities. Certainly, his Kirk Session was in uproar about it and Murdo's lack of "a good, solid Presbyterian rebuttal of these creatures of the devil".

Kiera tried hard to act normally and engage Murdo in conversation but Donald was struggling. Like a meerkat, his head would constantly look at the bathroom door or glance out the window in hope of some oncoming storm forcing the minister to leave early. His eyes were also on the shopping bags, full of fish and salt, that Kiera had arrived with. Soon the time of departure arrived.

"Well Kiera, we had best get going. Thank you for the tea but if we don't hurry Laura will give me a row for keeping you here. I'll just use your bathroom before I go if I may."

"No. You can't."

"Sorry Donald, why not?"

"It's impossible. You'll have to go outside." Donald was on his feet now reaching towards the door, ready to usher Reverend McKinney onto the grass outside.

"Are you out of your mind, Donald?"

"Donald, stop being silly, just because the toilet has that slight issue. Sorry Murdo but you won't have to use the grass. It's the flush system, not working properly." Donald's face went white.

"Excellent, I'll just pop and use it."

"Murdo, if you can just give me a hand first. You're tall and I need you to reach freshener in the kitchen for me. Donald, can you start clearing the bathroom please, I think I left some stuff in there." Murdo followed Kiera into the kitchen while Donald quickly opened the bathroom door and without hesitating grabbed the mermaid around the hips and threw her over his shoulder. She let out a low howl, like that of a seal before she was silenced abruptly as her head caught a shelf as Donald turned for the door. Regardless, he continued into the living room before tripping over his now empty cup of tea leaving his unconscious mermaid lying prostrate face up on the floor.

Hearing the commotion, Kiera brushed back past Murdo and suppressed a gasp on seeing her new boyfriend lying across a semi-naked fish lady. Reacting quickly, she turned on her heel assuring Murdo that Donald had just dropped something and pointed him in the direction of the highest shelf where she decreed the freshener must be.

Glancing back out of the kitchen, Kiera saw Donald pick up the mermaid and then fumble desperately with the bedroom door. With Murdo right behind her, she spun round quickly keeping him in the kitchen.

"Is Laura good?"

"Yes, yes. You can judge for yourself if we get going," said a bemused Murdo.

"Has she been okay with this fish business?" The end of the sentence rose in tone.

"Yes, I think so."

"But is she done and dusted with it? I mean really finished, Murdo. How does one know when we are finished with these things we have to do?"

"Kiera, I haven't got the faintest idea what you are on about. What do you mean finished with?"

"Bathroom's clear for you, Reverend," announced Donald

poking his head into the kitchen.

"But I haven't got the freshener yet."

"Never mind that, Murdo. We'd better get moving or Laura will be wondering where we are at. Best you visit the little boy's room sharp-ish." Murdo in total bemusement at the lurching conversation, gave up and did as ordered. Donald took hold of Kiera and whispered in her ear.

"What we going to do with her nibs? Can't leave her on her own."

"We're just going to have to. I'll lock the door and close the curtains all round. Just need to fill the bath again before we go out and add the salt. You'll need to keep Murdo occupied outside."

"We need to move her soon. Do you think she's ready to go back?"

"I don't know, Donald. We need to take her somewhere where we can see her swim but away from people seeing."

"Like a swimming pool."

"Yes," pondered Kiera, "the swimming pool." Murdo exited the bathroom and on seeing the couple close together strategically wandered over to Kiera's groceries, picking them up and announcing,

"What's with all the fish and salt, Kiera? Explains your bathroom mind, it reeks of fish."

"Just a good offer, Murdo. The salt's for doing a deep clean." Deciding the conversation was getting too surreal, Murdo didn't comment on the wet carpet nor how it was that Kiera didn't already have fish as Donald had been night fishing all week. Young people are getting beyond me now, thought Murdo, leaving the house.

Following Murdo out, Donald announced Kiera was just

sorting herself out and stood with Murdo in silence, a long standing, male, island tradition when awaiting the womenfolk. It took Kiera another ten minutes to lift the mermaid back, add salt to a running bath and then leave her enough fish to be getting on with. Donald's notion of the swimming pool was running around her mind and she began to see how this would work. But would Donald be up for a double-date?

# 10

# James

With the sun shining and a high tide rolling in, James was taking advantage of his two weeks off the ferry. Freed from the duties of attending to hungry deck hands, he now stood on the rocks down at one of the tiny lochs where the fish would swim by on occasion and the odd one would make a grab for the hook dangling off his line. There was nothing like this. A slight breeze in the face and a perfect mental calm, only the sound of the seagulls and the lapping of the waves.

Things had started to get a little silly with all this mermaid nonsense. Town was busy with extra tourists and no doubt when he returned to work, the runs would be much busier. He was glad he only served the crew as dealing with puking passengers and little kids chucking their sweets around was no way to attract any girls. Being stuck in the crew section didn't help either but at least he could get out on the deck occasionally to check out any talent that was travelling.

The one good bit of news regarding these mermaids was that the girls from the newspaper were coming to the island. Maybe they were worried about their jobs, thinking the mermaids would take over. Still, it would be good to see them in the flesh, so to speak. Especially that little brunette who was always in the paper. Yes, that was his favourite. Now, she could make a man happy. Well, James anyway, who cares about anyone else.

James cast his line into the sea and watched it unravelling, disappearing into the silvery-blue that reminded him of that android in the movies who could melt down and then reform. Imagine the sea doing that, the machine that formed would be massive. His line having stopped unravelling, James, with a practised ease, started to pull the rod up and then reel in quickly keeping the perk in motion through the water.

The line became tense and each pull took more effort. James licked the salt air from his lips. Got one, he thought. Gradually he pulled the perk closer and could see a faint silver blur in the water. A good one too judging the size from here. Within a minute, a fine pollack was exiting the water to be placed on the rock beside him. Taking his priest, James dispatched the fish before using his knife to gut it. Having been taught by his grandfather, he had no difficulty in filleting the fish, placing it in a cool-bag and then returning the guts back into the water. Well the day's not wasted, he thought.

"Anything biting?" James turned his head and saw Iain McClaren looking down from the rock's above. Although not one of James' friends, Iain's background and the loss of his Dad soo young was common knowledge amongst those of James' age.

"Wee pollack. Definitely some out there. Beautiful day."

"Suppose so."

James could see something sharp poking out from behind Iain's back. "Is that a new rod on your back?"

Iain stopped walking and came down close to James. "No.

It's not. Took me a while to get this, had to come from the mainland. Ain't she a beauty?"

James looked at the gun-type device Iain took off his back. It had a speared point on a metal shaft sticking out of the gun barrel and after a few seconds it dawned on James what he was looking at.

"What the hell are you hunting? Bit extreme for pollack."

"I got my rod for the pollack. No, this is for those filth that are coming up from the deep again. I'm going to get me a mermaid." James was about to burst out laughing but realised there was a man in front of him holding a harpoon and intent on hunting mythical creatures. He tempered his response.

"Really, wow. So, how are you going to get them?" Iain opened the haversack he was carrying. A variety of white fish was laid out, all gutted and obviously shop bought.

"It's not much I know but the stocks of fresh fish in the shops are very low. I'd do better with live ones but I got chased off the fish farms when I tried to get some."

"Have you used the harpoon before? Is there a big kick off it?"

"Well, takes a bit of getting used to. I haven't fired it much as I think people get a bit worried at it but it'll take something like this to take down a mermaid I reckon. Or even a merman."

"Merman! You reckon they have males?"

"Sure or how do they make wee ones? Nasty pieces of work no doubt. Wouldn't mind hauling one of them in. The harpoon's good but if I do get one I'll need to finish it off quick." Iain pulled a short handled mace from his bag. "My grandpa stole it from a museum years ago on the mainland. Bit rusty but it still works."

"You're certainly well equipped."

"You have to be prepared, these are strong. Pulled my Dad down into the deep before, so I doubt I'll go hunting them in a boat. Liable to get pulled clean off the deck. I'll stick to the rocks and cliffs. Bring them back to my territory."

"You'll need to be careful bringing them back on the land."

"How?"

"Don't they change? Get legs as soon as they're dry. It'll look like you're spearing a human. I mean, I don't know if the gills disappear or not. Could find yourself in a sticky situation."

"Hmm, you're right. I'll have to finish it in the shallows. Anyways, best get off hunting. Let me know if you see one."

"Will do." James gave a quick wave goodbye. He had no intention of alerting Iain if he saw a mermaid. Imagine the scene, the photos. The girls from the paper weren't going to be hanging about with that sort of nonsense going on. Dangerous clown, never right since he lost his dad.

The sun was out and the fishing was good. James stayed in the same spot until mid-afternoon when his bag was full of fish. Having gutted all the fish, he thought of how to dispose of them. Well, he could take a wee walk around his punters and pick up a bit of beer money. Reverend McKinney would be the nearest and Laura would always take a couple of fillets for her freezer. Might get a cup of coffee too. James tidied up his gear and started across the crofts for the manse.

A grey, dull yet vast building with copious unused rooms, the manse sat on top of a small hill overlooking its village. James was tired walking up to it and gratefully dropped his bag and rods on the doorstep before sounding the large, black knocker. The thuds rang into the house and James waited patiently until the door was pulled back revealing the diminutive minister's wife. As ever Laura showed first a look of surprise before her face slipped into its usually happy gait.

"James, good to see you. Been fishing?"

"Couple of lovely wee pollack Mrs McKinney, if you're interested. Just caught mind, well fresh. Thought of you first, always a warm welcome here."

"Excellent James. You'll come in of course, I have some guests from the mainland with me but you'll fit in just grand. Take the fish into the back and leave them in the fridge. Glass of wine for you?"

"Oh, wine, must be someone special."

"All my guests are special James, you know that." James smiled. Laura always made him feel welcome like his Auntie Cathy used to. It was six years now since she passed on and he missed going there for his Sunday dinner. On a quiet day, she was good fun.

James kicked off his boots and leaving them at the door, took six fillets through to Laura's kitchen. On passing her front room, he heard giggles and laughs of a female variety and he wondered who was there. James liked girls but was not very good at being "cool". Since leaving school, his time amongst the opposite sex was limited, especially as two weeks out of four were spent on the ferry. And anyway, he was always the quiet one in the pub, struggling for a word to say.

"Girls, this is my own personal fisherman, James." Surely this was a dream. James just stood there looking dumb as he took in the view around him. It was them. Right here, right now, in Laura's room. He knew Laura was a Godly woman but now he realised she was an angel. The blonde on the left, that was Candice. To her right, brunette, Debbie. Tanya, the redhead, Kyla, another blonde and then, oh yes, it must be.

Right in front of him was Alyssa.

She was dressed in a large t-shirt and jeans but still her curves showed through. With long, dangling waxy brown hair and teeth that looked like a dentist's advertisement, James thought she looked even better than her picture in the paper. Having spotted her last, his eyes didn't leave their post.

"James, say hello then."

"Hi."

"Sorry girls, I think us women are a bit too much for him. James grab a seat, there's room beside Alyssa. She's the one at the end."

"I know." James reddened. Heck, now she knows I check her out in the paper. And Laura knows. But I am getting to sit beside her. James was waiting to wake up from the dream.

"Are you really a fisherman, James?" asked Alyssa.

"She wants to know about your rod," Tanya chirped in. Alyssa threw her a snarled look before turning back to James.

"My dad used to fish James. I've always wanted to try but down in London there's not that much opportunity. At least I don't think so but up here it must be so good. Fancy taking a girl down the rocks?" asked Alyssa.

James sat there and stared at Alyssa, totally embarrassed and yet, in a most wonderful place. He wanted to be suave, sophisticated and above all charming. Despite failing at all of these, she had just asked him for a date. Well, a fish anyway. If only his mouth would work.

"He'd love to, Alyssa, wouldn't you James?" prompted Laura. James just nodded and began to beam. The other girls laughed but Alyssa smiled back in return.

The embarrassment was broken by the sound of the front door opening and a shout of "home" from the Reverend

McKinney. Laura leapt to her feet to see if anyone was with him and greeted Kiera and Donald in the hallway. Telling Murdo to take their coats, she dragged them into the front room and introduced their guests. The conversation began politely enough until the state of the mermaid's dress was brought up by Tanya.

"I don't see why the people here get into such a flap about the mermaids. We had those church people shouting at us, just because we go topless like the mermaids. I mean it's not like we were parading along the sea front. Spawn of the devil she called me. Can you imagine? Bloody church people."

"You're drinking bloody church people's wine," said Kiera.

"Now now, Kiera, Tanya has a point. I think spawn of the devil is wrong in all sorts of ways," said Laura.

"So you're okay with it. It is art after all. Not our fault if others get upset, is it?" asked Tanya.

"Well, I wouldn't go as far as that. It is your choice Tanya but personally I think your body is for your partner to see and enjoy," said Murdo, while his wife was gently shaking her head to silence him.

"That's a bit much. Laura, do you seriously go with that."

"Tanya, at my age there is little call for me to display anything," laughed Laura, "but in my day I had no issue with sunbathing topless abroad or wearing attractive things for my Murdo. Different places have different rules and when I was out in the Caribbean and the Americas and then Africa there were different degrees of dress. Outrageous in one place was normal in another. Ultimately it's your body but don't be ignorant of what you do to a man. Don't be ignorant of their reactions."

"Anyway," said Kiera, "I think we have a bit more to us than some advanced fish from the deep."

"But what about getting paid for it? My family, well my extended family, see my parents aren't around anymore, think I am selling myself, Laura. My aunt called me a prostitute," said Alyssa. James started shuffling uncomfortably. The word wasn't one he liked being associated with Alyssa who he had held in goddess form on the pages of the paper.

"Honestly dear, it wouldn't be for me. But it is up to you. I just think there's more to you all than a pair of boobs. What do you think Murdo?"

Murdo had been hoping to remain outside the conversation and like the rest of the men in the room was feeling distinctly uncomfortable with the direction it was heading. Oh well he thought, you pitched me in Laura so I hope you are okay with this.

"Well, my Laura is beautiful. When we were younger, she was a little stunner. But as she has aged, and she has aged better than me, her physical beauty isn't what it was. And I remember her beauty but it's not what Laura is or was, only a part. I got to know everything else about her and I still see her beauty as a person, as a lover still and as a friend. For as a good a body as she had, I would hate for her to be remembered at her funeral simply for having a nice pair of boobs. And she won't be. Whatever we put forward the world will engage with, some will use, some will bless and some will abuse. So in a roundabout way to an answer: as much as I and all us other guys love to look, the more you emphasize them, the more we just think you are them. Careful what you do."

James sat feeling a little embarrassed. His dream girl seemed to be in a modelling crisis and was working out if she was a prostitute. It was all going so well when fishing was on the agenda.

"Well, my boobs have got me to where I am today," said Tanya, "and I'm happy to show off what God gave me. Only natural after all."

Thank you Lord, thought Murdo, that this moment was not one upon which you felt the need to have the Kirk session intrude upon. He felt Laura squeeze his hand. This was not going to be the last debate on the outrageous mermaids.

# 11

# Mermaid Hunting

Leaving the bar door swinging behind him, Donald scanned for Kiera. She was sitting with Hayley, the veterinary student, in one of the darker corners of the bar. The bar was rather shabby with the occasional piece of flaked paint and ripped coverings on the stools. Often quiet during the week, it could get lively on a weekend and was considered one of the social venues to be in. Donald wasn't a keen visitor of pubs and he had been babysitting the mermaid while Kiera sought out help for their house guest. It was time to swap roles.

The young couple had decided that before trying to reacquaint the mermaid with the sea again, they should let her get used to swimming in a more protected environment. Donald had come up with the idea of using the local swimming pool but Kiera had seen how to do it. Her friend, Hayley, had started going out with the assistant manager of the facilities and his boss was away for the next two weeks. As the pool was closed on Sundays, Kiera needed to convince Hayley that she should try for a late Saturday night rendezvous with her man at the pool. An after-hours special to which Donald and herself would double-date. Once in, they would produce the extra guest.

Kiera had spent an evening working on Hayley and the idea seemed to be a runner. Hayley had phoned Tommy, her boyfriend, and after initial protestations he took the bait when Hayley mentioned some night swimming, possibly al fresco. As Donald approached, the two girls were giggling.

"Hello my lover," greeted Kiera. Donald saw the two empty bottles of wine on the table. Oh heck.

"Hi. Are you ready or do you want longer?"

"Donald, my Donald. Just telling my mate Hayley here, he's super Hayley, that you need a pair of speedos. One of those skimpy pairs for our little get together."

"Oh, Kiera, you ever seen him in speedos?" laughed Hayley.

"Seen his legs. Yes, I have seen his legs and those thighs. Yummy, Hayley, they are yummy. He's just gorgeous, my gorgeous babe. That right Donald." Oh boy, thought Donald, this could be a taxi job.

"Anything for you, Kiera. Are we all systems go for tomorrow?" Donald's patience was wearing thin already.

"Donald, I shall be delighted to join you and your speedos tomorrow night for a little night swimming. I think Kiera may just have the hots for you." Hayley raised her glass with aplomb and let her blonde hair swing round her shoulders. Although she was a larger girl than Kiera, Hayley had the curves that carried her figure, looking buxom rather than overweight.

"Are you ready for the bikini sisters, Donald?" asked Kiera. Flippin' heck thought Donald, here we go. Trying to get the mermaid some sensible recuperation in the pool and Kiera's got Hayley thinking it's a snog-in. Hope she reacts positively when we turn up with our guest.

"Think the ladies need to go home and get some sleep. After all, a big night ahead tomorrow, you don't want to be meeting these wonderful men with baggy eyes and sore heads." The girls jeered briefly but accepted their coats from Donald as he ushered them outside towards the taxi ranks. Hayley stopped him at one point and grabbed his cheeks with her hands placing her face right in front of Donald's.

"Donald, you have lips of fire. Kiera says they are so hot. Oh Donald, you take care of my girl, you hear me. Or I'll sort you out. I'll do you. I'll....." Hayley began to fall but Donald grabbed her.

"Donald, hands off, you have Kiera. I may look like a siren but I'm meant for another. I'm...." Hayley half-fell, half-ran behind a nearby wall before emptying most of her dinner from that evening. This mermaid better be thankful, thought Donald. Heck, it's right down her front.

Twenty minutes later, Donald had cleaned up Hayley, dodged her accusations of his cleaning activities as a front to get his hands on her cleavage and had then sent her home in a taxi. Kiera was sat on a wall, watching him wave goodbye to Hayley.

"Donald, I'm drunk."

"Yes, you are." Donald smiled. Despite her current inebriation, Kiera still looked stunning. He knew he was smitten. She sat with her head slightly down and her dark hair slightly obscuring her face.

"Are you fit to look after her?" asked Donald.

"Donald.....she's in a bath and has no legs, where's she gonna go?"

"I'll get you a taxi." He waved his hand at the nearby rank and turned to Kiera. She intercepted him with a deep kiss.

"Argggh, Kiera. Peach snaps too, you were on peach snaps!

Flippin' disgusting." Kiera licked her lips.

"Well, you tasted okay." With a peck on his cheek, she clambered into a taxi and watched him out of the rear view window as it disappeared. How long would this feeling last, she wondered? At least until tomorrow, she told herself.

Donald returning to the bar was intercepted by Tommy, Hayley's new boyfriend. Recognising him from the leisure center, Tommy looked just as smart in his jeans and striped shirt. Donald didn't know him that well but like everyone from the island, they had been in secondary school around the same time.

"Donald, you wee dancer. How did you get Kiera onto that idea? Private swimming. Hayley's gonna wear her bikini. She was even talking about the sauna or steam room." Donald did wonder if he displayed anything like the excitement a man should when faced with a night with his beloved, near enough alone and in amorous circumstances. But all he could think was, there will be an incredible smell of fish, how are we going to get rid of that?

"Well, she's not behind the door."

"And nabbing her in the first place, you dark horse, sir. Well done mate, bloody well done. Once we get shut up tomorrow, just come down. I'll buy some wine and that. Hell Donald, my loins are on fire!"

Donald smiled at his forwardness but didn't want to get drawn any further on the subject. So he bought Tommy a pint but made his excuses to leave. Part of him saw only disaster for the venture but Kiera had been so positive once he had had the initial idea. Kiera had teased him about what she should wear, whether her swimsuit or her thong. Except for her showing him, Donald would have doubted she had a thong. Whilst the idea was an enjoyable one, he had reservations about other people being present. Needs must though.

The night was calm and there was a slight cooling breeze off the sea. This inspired Donald into taking a walk home despite the considerable distance involved. So often he was stuck on the ferry on such nights and unable to fully enjoy the sea air by exercising his lungs with a brisk walk. On this particular two weeks of time off, he had not been getting out at all what with the mermaid and being with Kiera. Despite being thankful for her intervention, he wished the mermaid was gone and his relationship with Kiera could have some normality about it, maybe even some late night walks.

The moon was bright and almost full which caused a silvery reflection on the sea, highlighting the minor ripples it now displayed. There were things about this island he would change, things he could almost curse, but nights like these were the treasure of this place. Part of him mourned not having his rod and line with him for a quiet night's fishing. Once his pinnacle, it now ran a close second to a quiet night with Kiera.

The peace and the calm allowed Donald a place to think and reflect on this mad week gone by. Tomorrow night could be a disaster but would definitely be a watershed. At last others would know and the secret they had carried together would be exposed. Donald was worried that with the mermaid gone and the excitement of this adventure dissipated, would Kiera still be so keen on him? Was this a fling of excitement, or the start of a life's journey? Either way, there was no backing out, for Kiera was worth a risk.

After an hour's walk and contemplation, Donald was heading towards the jetty where he had first found his stricken mermaid. Instinctively, he meandered towards the spot he had first seen her but froze suddenly on hearing some encouraging but directive words.

"And turn up. Lift that head. Beautiful. Just stunning girl. Now pout. Lovely. And smile. Cracker-jack, girl. Bingo!"

He tried to be casual but, in reality, he woodenly walked over to the wall at the harbour, seeking refuge while he ascertained who was ahead. He had an idea and was already feeling awkward. Donald juked quickly over the wall and had his suspicions confirmed. Two men were standing on the shore, one with a camera and one holding what looked like a large reflective shade. The man with the camera was unknown to Donald but the other man was his work colleague James. In front of them, knee deep in the sea was Alyssa, the model he had met at the McKinneys'.

James was wearing a broad smile on his face but otherwise was standing, looking positively dumb-struck. Repeated flashes of light lit up the brunette girl whose hair was now more curled than that afternoon. She had a green strapped bikini top of two sea-shells and wore a fish tail from the waist down. Her body had been greased up, possibly with goose fat which gave her the same translucent skin as Kiera's house guest. Donald ducked back down and considered his options.

He could just hide until they were done. If he was discovered, he would look like some sort of pervert who had been spying on Alyssa from behind the wall. Alternatively, he could leap out from behind the wall and say hello. This idea was better except Donald wasn't too sure what he would say. "Lovely evening for it" didn't seem all that appropriate. Would he ask James what he was doing here? If asked back, what would he say? Having a sea inspired refreshing walk at one in the morning didn't seem all that believable, even if it was the truth.

"Okay, Alyssa, uncover. Lovely girl, just lovely. And lean forward."

Oh bugger, thought Donald sitting tight against the wall. If I pop out now it's just going to be downright embarrassing. It's not like I'll be able to just look her in the face. I'll try but it's not going to happen. He recalled seeing Kiera "al fresco" as he preferred to call it and the embarrassment and the pleasure. No. One woman was enough. Well there was the mermaid too. Not that she was an item but there was those as well. Dammit, life was simpler just going back and forth on the ferry without this female beauty assault to endure.

There was a reflection in the water at the end of the harbour wall. As his eyes adjusted, Donald could make out a small boat silently skirting the end of the pier with a figure standing upright. In its arms was a metallic object the top of which was glinting in the moonlight. Carefully, the figure was raising this metallic object and Donald suddenly saw an arrowhead at the front of the device. His brain screamed the word weapon at him just as he heard a pressure release and saw the arrowhead disappear.

Alyssa screamed. In agony. Uncontrolled, pain induced yelling that ripped through the air. There was the sound of a man leaping out of his boat and stomping through the water, calling aloud for vengeance on these "damned bitches of the sea." James could be heard shouting at this intruder and racing into the fray. Donald raced round from the wall to see this woman of beauty lying face down in the sea with a harpoon speared through her right shoulder.

The assailant was wielding a knife and kept pulling on the

harpoon line with his other hand causing the stricken girl to twist in the sea. Donald headed to cut off the madman but James was beating him to it. Without halting, James launched himself square into the boatman and met his forehead with the man's nose. His body carried through emptying the man off his feet and sending both crashing into the water. As Donald reached them, James had the man by the scruff of the neck and was pummeling him with punches to the face.

"Bastard, I'll kill you." Donald saw the boatman was stone cold from the beating and urged James to calm down. James rounded off another frenzy of punches before he would stop and Donald caught the boatman's head as James let him drop to the sea. Running back to Alyssa, James took her from the photographer's arms, holding her awkwardly as the harpoon would allow. Donald dragged the boatman with his bloodied face back to shore, recognising him now as Iain McClaren, the boy who lost his father to mermaids. Oh hell, thought Donald.

The photographer was busy tapping in 999 to his phone and then repeating it. He looked at Donald asking where the signal was and Donald realised they were in trouble. He looked desperately for something to cut the harpoon line and had to search back in the water for the assailant's knife. James yelled at him to hurry while the photographer started to cry and become incoherent. Spying the knife in the water, Donald cut the line and told James to pick Alyssa up.

"Where do we go? Where, Donald, bloody where? She's dying, there's pissing blood everywhere."

"Up the hill to Kiera's. She's done first aid. She's got a phone. Bring Alyssa. I'll go on ahead. Camera guy, watch that guy, tie his hands, keep him quiet"

"Just kill the bastard," yelled James.

"That's not helping Alyssa, James. Hurry. Just hurry. Follow me. Come on."

# 12

# Aftermath

It had been one hell of a night and as he watched the sun rise from his vantage point at the rear of Kiera's cottage, Donald began to wonder what drove people to such violence. Iain's story was well known and had been widely dismissed up until now. Even with the sighting of the mermaids off the ferry, his tale was still disbelieved. Iain clearly believed though.

An arm hugged him around the waist and he felt a gentle kiss on the neck and a tight embrace. Kiera had been so calm when it had happened. James had carried Alyssa in her half-naked state and placed her on the couch screaming at Kiera to help. And she had. Stemming the flow of blood, she put her training as a nurse to good use. Despite only having a few hours of sleep from Donald leaving her, the situation soon forced a sober head. When the ambulance arrived she was cool, informing the paramedics of Alyssa's condition and responses. Donald had been impressed as she ordered him about for all the necessary things to attend to the young woman's wound.

The mermaid had slept through it all and only Donald had entered the bathroom for water and towels. This hadn't been deliberate as Alyssa's wounds had taken priority but

Donald pondered how fortunate they had been. The police on arrival had taken brief statements at the door and then made for the hospital to interview James, who had accompanied Alyssa in the ambulance. The secret was intact but Donald was convinced their guest needed to be moved out as soon as possible.

Kiera was shaking as she held him. He turned and held her face with his hands looking into frightened eyes. There was a slight welling of tears and she buried her face into his neck.

"You were amazing, Kiera. You probably saved her life."

"It was just the training. God Donald, how do you do that to someone? To anything?"

"I know. Just don't Kiera. You won't understand. He's got issues. He's just not right."

"She'll not model again. Daft like, thinking about that when she could have been dead. But it's true, she won't."

"James would have killed him, Kiera. He smashed his face to pieces before I could stop him. Camera guy just fell apart. What a bloody mess."

"Get me a cuppa, would you? And the duvet from my room. I want to just sit on my bench and watch the sunrise. I need to see something good."

Donald nodded and went to the kitchen. He ground the beans and then allowed the filter to work before taking two steaming mugs back out to the bench. Kiera had stretched out on the bench but her eyes were red from crying. She reached out for the mugs and thanked Donald before reminding him of the duvet. It took a moment for him to register as he was taken aback by how much Kiera was reeling from the events. During the chaos she had seemed so strong and now she was just a wreck. And he loved her for her brokenness for others.

They spent two quiet hours under the duvet occasionally kissing, more for reassurance than from passion. Right there Donald decided to tell his mother of his desire for Kiera. He knew she wouldn't approve, worried that Kiera would eventually take him away from the island and would complain that she was Catholic, not fully saved or whatever. And how that would affect the kids? What kids, he wasn't even married yet? All he knew was he was hook, line and sinker into Kiera and he no longer cared what anyone else thought about it.

"There's you two. Are you okay?" Laura's cheery voice broke the quiet.

"No, Laura, no." Kiera's answer restored the silence. Laura sat down on the bench beside them and stared out to the sea. She had seen too many people in shock and grief to interrupt the therapeutic moments of peace they required. It was a full ten minutes before she spoke again.

"Murdo's up at the hospital. They called him in his capacity as chaplin, Alyssa had asked for him. She's going to be okay. They were very complimentary of you both, especially your work Kiera. You two did good however bad the situation feels."

"How's James?" asked Donald.

"Murdo said he was good. Very attentive to Alyssa. Apparently they couldn't move him all night. You two should pay her a visit."

"Well Laura, she probably needs some time to heal. I expect her family will be up on the plane soon as," said Kiera.

"She's got no one. Been in foster care since she was nine apparently. It's amazing what people will tell Murdo. He's got a gift for it."

"Well, we'll get up there soon. Just as soon as Kiera's ready. It's been a bit much."

"Good. And don't worry about any dinner or that. I brought some stuff and dropped it into your kitchen, Kiera. Just micro it. You need sleep too."

"I don't think I'll get much today, Laura. We have to go to the police station too this morning. Give out statements. I take it Iain's in the cells," said Kiera.

"No, he's at the hospital too. Still spitting blood for the mermaids. Apparently his face is a mess and he's had to have stitches." They sat in silence a bit longer. Soon Kiera asked for more coffee and Donald made a point of kissing her deeply before retiring to the kitchen. Laura smiled her response before telling Kiera she was lucky to have Donald. Kiera nodded. She wanted to tell Laura all about her new found love but the morning's events sat heavy on her mind. Why is there never a perfect moment on this earth? There's always some darkness to spoil it.

An hour later, Murdo arrived and gave them a lift to the police station. The officers were polite and compassionate but their job and attention to detail required several hours of going over statements before the couple could leave the station. They caught the bus to the hospital and found their access to Alyssa blocked as she was having further treatment. Finding the cafeteria, they satisfied their hungry stomachs before returning to Alyssa's ward.

An hour ago, the corridor to the ward had been empty but now it was packed with reporters. A horde of flashguns suddenly exploded and a reporter shoved a microphone in Kiera's face asking if she knew the page three model and if she thought she was attacked in a crime of beauty. Kiera doubted she even understood the question and felt a rage build up inside her that this person could be so rude as to accost someone coming to visit an ill person. Donald saw her shoulders rise and immediately grabbed her hand dragging her through the crowd. Nurse MacKenzie, who had been so good with his mother when she had that trouble (women's things and Donald asked no further), was waving at him through the slightly open door and he fixed his eyes on her and dragged his girlfriend through.

"Thanks Mrs Mackenzie, where did they come from?" said Donald.

"Donald, and this must be Kiera. Well done girl. You may just have saved her life between the pair of you. Nasty wound, very nasty. Crazy thing sitting there topless on a rock that time of night, catch yourself a cold to chill you to death. Ah, well shouldn't say such things, she was the victim, didn't deserve that nonsense anyway." Kiera had been looking for a place to say hello but Donald having previous experience, had remained quiet knowing no opportunity would emerge from the long grass.

"It was nothing." Kiera felt a small measure of triumph fitting in this brief sentence during Mrs MacKenzie's slight pause for breath.

"Nothing, nonsense girl, you should have stayed in the business with hands like that. Anyway, young James has been with her all night. Poor lad is shattered. She's going to be moved to the mainland for a few days to get some further work on her shoulder. The scarring's fairly extensive and her career might be in jeopardy they reckon. So take it easy with her, no mention of getting back to work. She's lucky to be alive."

"Blessed," said Donald, "blessed."

"Can we see her?" asked Kiera.

"Of course. She said she hoped you would be here and James told Murdo to ask for you. He's very good that Rev McKinney, despite all they say about him and his modern ways. One to one he's hard to beat. A fair regular up here and nearly all happy to see him. Not that I've heard him preach mind."

"Sunday mornings and evenings," said Kiera suppressing a wicked smile.

"Which room?" interjected Donald quickly.

"This way dears. Of course nothing I have said leaves this ward. Those vultures will be all over you when you leave."

Alyssa was lying down when they entered her room. In the corner was a large basket of fruit and flowers with a logo of the paper she posed for spread across the bottom. The room was bright but smelt of hospital disinfectant and at her side was one of those pay for view televisions. In the corner by the window was a strong armchair, cream in colour with beech arms and legs. Its occupant was asleep and snoring loudly. As Kiera moved round to the bottom of the bed Alyssa's eyes opened wide.

"You came."

"Yes," said Kiera, "we had to go to the police station first but then we came straight up. They were dealing with you so we grabbed lunch while we waited."

"How you feeling?" asked Donald.

Alyssa looked away out the window before turning her eyes to James. Then she studied the drip beside her.

"I don't know. I really don't know." Kiera rushed forward and held her tight as Alyssa burst into tears. All Kiera could do was hold her and tell her she was safe. After a few minutes Alyssa sniffed hard and started apologising.

"I'm sorry. It's just all so..... sudden. Nothing's sure now.

The paper called but all the editor wanted was a feature. My story. What I felt like? Was it my body he was attacking? Am I like the mermaids? Did I think he had a problem with women? Was there anything sexual? Don't they get it?" yelled Alyssa," I don't give a shit! I just want to be on my own."

Kiera let the following silence lie, nodding her affirmation instead. Alyssa looked out the window again and Donald felt a deep empathy for her situation. No longer the center of attention for her glamour, she was now to be the freak attacked, the hunted prey, her control of her sexuality destroyed. And those who paid her wage were the ones pushing it.

"I won't model again. The consultant said so. This shoulder won't work properly and there's a high likelihood my shoulders will look different. My boobs won't matter with lob sided shoulders."

"Let's just take it one day at a time," said Kiera, "try and be positive. You're a gorgeous lass and there's a guy there who risked his life for you and hasn't left you since. There's girls would kill for that. If it wasn't for Donald, I'd be jealous."

"I know but it's all pretty crazy. Damn I don't know. But look, thank you, thank you both. I might have been dead but for you two and James. He's been so good. They fly me away soon. But when that's done I said I want to recuperate up here, not back in London. You guys will visit?" Donald and Kiera nodded. "Good. Not sure I can stand the girls telling me how my career will be over. I love them but it's all they will talk about. That vicar and his wife, you guys and my James here, you're more positive. I could do with that." Well she's no bimbo, thought Donald.

Kiera's mobile vibrated in her pocket. By instinct she pulled it out and glanced at it. There was a text message from Hayley asking if they were still on tonight. Alyssa laughed when Donald told Kiera not to be so rude and then became interested when Kiera said Hayley was asking if Donald's trunks were a go-er. Donald went crimson red as Kiera described their elicit double date but left out the fifth guest at the party. As they left the ward by the rear entrance to avoid the press at the main door, Donald became agitated.

"Kiera, if the press know then we have to move her asap. They are bound to pick up our role in all this and they'll be knocking your door."

"Easy Tiger. We just go back to mine, lock the door and get a bit of sleep. If they are there, we'll give them a wee statement and then say we'll be going to bed. Once it's properly dark we'll get her out and down to the pool. They'll not be expecting that."

"I just have a bad feeling about this. It's all starting to get a bit mad."

"Donald, I love you to bits, I so do but I'm going to be in a bikini tonight and I'll take any attempt to get out of this as a slur on my body." It was unfair and it took Donald a few seconds before he realised she was joking. She put him on edge sometimes. It was one of the things he really liked about her.

# 13

# Catching Your Man

Murdo was tired. The hospital visiting in the middle of the night and the extreme situation he had found were more than he was used to. Between helping Alyssa and James, he had been ferrying Laura about and dealing with fending off reporters who had spotted him as the religious involvement in last night's drama. Hoping he had been sensible and respectful with his answers, Murdo had beat a retreat and sought the quiet of his front room to prepare both of tomorrow's sermons. No rest for the wicked.

"All God's creatures" kept running through his mind and as he spent a little time in prayer, he sensed a honing of his message to the congregation. The incident was bound to send shock waves through the village as everyone knew the assailant to some capacity. He also knew Alyssa would be seen as getting her just desserts from many for "parading herself" in such a fashion. Poor girl. It didn't look like her shoulder would be able to be fixed properly and what with the deep scarring, she was unlikely to take up her former job. Murdo was not against this outcome but he certainly wouldn't have endorsed the method.

Taking a sip of coffee, Murdo found it had gone cold. A glance of the clock confirmed he had made it an hour ago. Oh well, tomorrow may have to be prepared in the head and not paper. Holy inspiration, he prayed.

The doorbell sounded. Dread filled up in Murdo's mind as he could guess who had rung the bell. It was bound to be that Mackenzie man and his side-kick MacIver. Blast it, is there no way to have an afternoon's peace and quiet? Shoulders drooping, Murdo plodded his way to the front door and tried to give a courteous hello to the most feared duo from his kirk session. He failed. Instead it came across as a "What do you want?"

"Minister, I am here representing your kirk session and indeed for the good of your whole congregation."

"Well Iain, matters must be pressing. What can I do for you?"

"No, minister, you misunderstand, it's what we can do for you."

"Ah, excellent. The back garden's in need of a cut. I have the petrol mower in the back, should be...."

"No, minister. Be serious."

"Oh, I was."

"This mermaid encounter. You are neglecting your duty. Tarnishing the Lord's name by associating with such ladies of the night." Murdo raised his eyebrows. "Racing on her command in the middle of the night and then not condemning her outright in front of the world's media for her actions."

"Iain, she got harpooned. By one of our own. An island lad. One who has been ostracised and placed on the edge because we called him mad to believe in such thing as mermaids. And that's a conclusion that has seriously been put into doubt."

"But minister, the reputation of this denomination and indeed, our own church, unsullied for years past is being put into doubt by your reckless actions and I am here to tell you to desist."

"You are here to do what?" thundered Murdo. He was tired, he was probably irritable but he certainly wasn't as irrational as what he was hearing.

"Your position as our minister is seriously in trouble if you carry on with this nonsense. The world is looking in at us and needs to be given an example. An example of genuine, wholesome religion."

"Pure religion is looking after orphans and widows."

"Exactly not these escorts, these loose women."

"Mr MacKenzie, now listen good. One, she is an orphan. Two, she is in need of help. Three, she asked for help. To ignore her cries would just not be Christian."

"I am just a poor sinner and I do not understand why you would take sides with this hooker while leaving the reputation of your flock to flounder. I am calling an emergency meeting of our kirk, sir and fully intend to remove you from your place of prominence."

Murdo took a deep breath as he was finding himself losing control. He looked past Mackenzie out towards the sea, wondering why the mermaids were wanting to show up here, why the equilibrium was being disturbed. Then he looked back into the face of his session clerk and found a reason.

"Do what you will. I will try and do what He would do. If that's not suitable for you then take it up with Him."

"How dare you put yourself in God's place. This is outrageous."

"Yes," said Murdo, "it is. It's called the gospel and He is the mark we are all called to."

"Maybe minister, but to suggest we are capable of living like Him. I've never heard such blasphemy."

"Read your bible, Iain. Find Him. And stop this crass attempt for self-importance."

"How dare you? I will not have this. Not on my watch." And the indignant Mr MacKenzie and the silent but still affronted Mr MacIver departed with much head shaking and huffing.

Oh well, thought Murdo, there is freedom, maybe even life without a kirk session. He knew the threat was real but it wouldn't be a unanimous feeling amongst the whole congregation. Most would actually agree with his actions but he knew the house of cards they all lived in, how image was king and thought his expulsion was a strong possibility. Laura would be excited though. She'd always thought they should be freer in their lives for God. Maybe she'll get her wish.

Kiera was not used to meeting people on street corners at midnight. She was also not used to wearing a bikini under a sweatshirt and track bottoms in the later hours of the day. Although it was early spring, the nights were still nippy and she felt quite cold waiting for Hayley. The town had its fair share of late night stragglers, making their way home from the pubs, denied a last pint beyond closing. There were occasional shouts and songs from those who on a sober night would know better.

Donald was causing her worry. Since the attack, his attitude to their guest had been much more somber and he was keen to move her on. The adrenalin rush of their combined discovery and new found passion had taken a darker tinge and although they were still feeling these new and strong urges about each other, the shine had been taken off.

Never during her time training as a first aider had Kiera expected to deal with anything soo bloody. Now as she stood in the quiet, images of dark red oozing from Alyssa's shoulder came back to haunt her. Her training had been good and had taken over during the incident. She had been praised for her handling of the wound and credited for Alyssa's survival. Yet part of her felt cold, weary and somewhat distant. Even with Donald, she was struggling to express what she was going through. But she could see the darkness in his own eyes, crushing the joy in him as it was in her.

Then Hayley was in her face.

"I went with the skimpy one just in case he thinks about backing out."

"Sorry, what?"

"Come on girl, you were miles away. I said I'm going to give that boy a night he'll never forget."

Well thought Kiera, I can promise that without the aid of a bikini.

"This is so subversive Kiera. You are a dark horse. I knew you were a bit different from us on the island but midnight swims and rendezvous, girl you are something else."

Alyssa, her shoulder busted, poor girl.

"We should go," said Hayley, "don't want to miss this just because we ran late. Is Donald on his way?"

"Donald? Oh, yes. He's coming along."

"Are you okay? This will be the same Donald you have been drooling and gassing about all last night to me. I thought you had it bad for him. Practically had you married off."

"Yes .... yes, Donald will be here. He's great, Hayley, just great. It's just last night. Was all a bit rough."

"God girl, I'm sorry. Getting caught up in myself here. If you want to cancel, I understand. I'll just make it a one-on-one."

"No! No, probably what I need, some distraction."

"And a little Donald loving," laughed Hayley.

And to be rid of one mermaid, thought Kiera.

Arriving at the front door of the leisure center, Hayley started waving frantically towards the shadows. A tall, muscular man stepped forward, dressed casually in a fleece and track bottoms. Although he glanced briefly at Kiera, his eyes then focused fully on Hayley and his lips moved into a broad smile. His hands were shaking slightly and he kept stepping from foot to foot. I hope this doesn't make him freak out, thought Kiera.

"Hi T," said Hayley, "You ready to party."

Please never let me call Donald "D", thought Kiera, surely I can be more imaginative than that.

"Hey baby."

Oh come on thought Kiera, suppressing a laugh. She dipped her head as the couple met and embraced, exploring each other's mouths for some thirty seconds.

"Where's Donald?" asked Tommy on finishing their kissing. Presumably all saliva had been expunged.

"On his way. He said he'd be slightly delayed and text me when he was outside."

"Okay, we'd better get inside before we get seen," said Tommy. He took a large number of keys, kept together on a ring, from his pocket and proceeded to fumble with them until he produced a single, silver one with some blue tape attached to the top. At the third attempt, he managed to make the key fit and opened the door to the center. Racing inside, he keyed in a code to silence any alarms and waved at the girls with a hurry up command. Once they were inside he locked the door again.

"So Hayley, is it the sauna and steam room we're going to use?" asked Tommy. Hayley giggled.

"Actually Tommy," said Kiera, "could we use the pool too?"

"The pool? Heck Kiera, that's a lot of work getting it ready. The safety covers on it and everything."

Blast, thought Kiera, he's not going to go for this. Think girl. Think. We're going to need that pool ready for Donald's arrival. There'll be no point having a stand up argument whilst holding a mermaid. Ah, thought Kiera.

"But skinny dipping's better in a pool Tommy. Don't you think?" She really did think he was going to faint. His jaw dropped and Kiera could see him questioning had she really just said that.

"Kiera!" said Hayley.

"What's the matter?" asked Kiera. "Once he sees that bikini he's going to want more. Come on Tommy, you ready to go kit off?"

"Yes .... yes, definitely, sure.... the pool, no problem Kiera, the pool." Tommy looked at Hayley in terrified hope.

"Go on lover, get it ready," laughed Hayley, "we'll get changed and I'll pour some wine. No point going half-ers on a night like this."

Kiera breathed a sigh of relief as Tommy almost ran to sort the pool out. Grabbing Kiera by the arm, Hayley gave her a cheeky look and dragged her towards the changing rooms. There were no lights on and Kiera at times thought she could see things moving in the dark. Part of her kept remembering Alyssa, in her exposed state, being attacked and a little trepidation crept in as they neared the cubicles.

Hayley, on the other hand, was bouncing with excitement. She removed two bottles of bubbly from her bag before cursing under her breath.

"What's up?" asked Kiera.

"No glasses. Damn, I had this all planned."

"Like he's going to notice the lack of glassware. Get in there and come out stunning."

Kiera forced an encouraging smile hoping Hayley didn't see her worry underneath. Donald still hadn't rung her phone. When they had been out that day, she had had some phone calls with messages left by various news outlets. This would be the worst time for them to look for an interview.

Changing out of her sweats, Kiera was quickly in her bikini. She hadn't worn it before, purchased by her older sister for a holiday she was booked on with both of her siblings. At the time, she thought it was outrageous and had no intentions of wearing it, preferring to hide herself in a swimsuit. As it happened, her younger sister broke her leg two weeks beforehand and they had cancelled, and so far hadn't rearranged. The heating in the center had been switched off now for three hours and there was definite chill across her skin as she undressed. Stepping out of the cubicle, her phone started to ring.

"Donald, where are you?"

"Got trouble Kiera. I just spent the last hour fending off the press."

"Is everything still okay?"

"Yeah. So far. I told them I was going home and you were at your uncle's."

"But he's dead. Well, Uncle Declan is, as for Seamus, he's in Canada."

"Kiera, I didn't actually think you would be going to them. Was just trying to get these clowns off out tail."

"Oh yeah, sorry."

"I may be a while but I am coming. It's too hot for her to stay here. Keep them occupied for me."

"Is that Donald?" asked Hayley emerging from her cubicle.

"Yes," replied Kiera, then sunk into silence as Hayley's full figure came into view. All Kiera could think was how she was going to keep Tommy sorting out the pool once he saw Hayley. She was practically ready to skinny dip as it was.

"Hand him over," instructed Hayley. Before she could argue Hayley had grabbed the phone, placed an arm around Kiera and set the device up to take a selfie of the pair of them. A few presses later and an image was on its way to Donald.

"Donald, it's Hayley."

"Oh, right. Hi there Hayley."

"Did you get the image?"

"No. Oh hang Hayley. Just in. Oh....."

"Like it Donald? ...... Donald, do you like it?"

"Yeah, well ......... wow. I mean both of you, wow. Well, obviously Kiera mainly. Not that you don't look.... but yeah, wow."

"Get here Donald, she's hot for you!" Hayley laughed as Kiera grabbed the phone back.

"Donald, you there?" asked Kiera.

"Yes Kiera. Here."

"Good. Just get here. I'll be.... here." This was tricky now Hayley was listening. She could probably only hear my half of the conversation but Donald probably doesn't realise.

"Okay Kiera. Be as quick as I can but no promises."

"Be quick. Please"

"Sure. Oh and Kiera. I so wish I didn't have a mermaid with me. You look so beautiful. Wow, girl. Just wow. Bye."

"Bye." Kiera took the phone from her ear and smiled to herself. I wish so too Donald. I wish so too.

# 14

# Handling the Livestock

They had seen her on the rocks, fifty meters from their boat. Although it was dark, the moonlight caught her pale skin against the rich, red hair. Swishing occasionally behind her, the tail was as evident as the subtle song she was singing. The captain thought of hearing the whale sounds on the wild life programme but with a somewhat softer and higher pitch. For the last thirty minutes they had stared silently from the boat, caught up in a wondrous mix of sheer disbelief in her appearance and captivation of her form.

Times had been hard for the master of the small fishing boat. Indeed, he was out checking creels this late in desperation. The bank manager had warned him that his overdraft would be recalled unless some signs of positive growth of his "business" were shown. Business! This was his livelihood, this was his passion. All he had ever known was the sea and its bounty, just as his father and grandfather had known. All of them had known fallow times but these last few years were the worst ever and the threat of looking for something on-shore was now becoming a reality. Well, the sea may take him before that happened.

But instead she had been gracious. Once again she had opened up her depths to provide him with the catch to sustain one who worshipped daily at her tides. The mermaid before him would provide not just a monetary solution but would guarantee him fame like his forefathers had never known. All that stood between him and preservation was the catch. For the last half hour he had been thinking how to bring in this beauty.

At first, he thought he could simply kill her. On board he had a small rifle and he thought about letting go a shot to the head. Would any of the vultures he would present her to really be bothered that their meat wasn't live? The taste of observing the unknown would be sated either way. But the thought of a missed shot combined with denying his skill as a fisherman, made him give up on that course. No, he would catch her, net her and present a live specimen for all to marvel at. In the morning light at the harbour's edge in front of the world's press, he would have his glory.

The small mackerel was bait on the large hook, hanging from his hand and the boat drifted silently closer. She seemed unaware of their presence with the wind blowing away from them and continued her song until a small fish landed beside her. Whether curiosity, hunger or foolishness, the mermaid immediately picked up the fish and bit into it. A large hook emerged through her cheek and her song changed to a wail.

"Quick boys, pull her in. She may rip her own cheek to escape."

Pulling hard against them, the mermaid fought for grip on the rocks. Her powerful tail flapped uselessly on the dry surface and there seemed to be a lack of muscular definition in her resisting arms. Quickly she fell backward and was dragged into the water.

The men in the boat were almost dragged overboard as the resistance increased. The line was tied to the wheelhouse of the boat and looped round the largest deckhand who was a balding figure, some six foot two in height and sported a bushy beard. The other charge was holding on in this grim tug of war, gloves protecting his hands from rope burns and feet planted against the boat's edge. The Captain stood at the front surveying the dark waters for signs of his catch and directing when to pull and when to release.

The boat was dragged toward the rocks making the Captain fear for its breaching but then the mermaid turned towards the open sea and began to pull the boat out. All three men were astounded at the speed with which the boat left the small inlet they had found her in and began to panic. The thought of the mermaid diving deep and tipping the boat worried the Captain and he decided to throw out the anchor behind him. There was no difference for the first half minute. Then the anchor caught and the boat's manoeuvres came to a sudden halt and the tension in the line grew harder.

"Let her fight boys, let her fight. She'll tire in a moment and then we'll pull her in."

It was four minutes before there was any slackness in the line. The Captain remained focused, for on sight of the mermaid's momentary rest, he yelled at his boys to pull. And pull hard. Slowly the line came and they dragged her in. There were brief moments of parity but she was losing, she was caught and her doom complete. The Captain smiled watching his crew reel in, his status and livelihood renewed.

There was no warning. It just leapt out of the water in front of the boat on the Captain's right hand side. A tail caught him powerfully about the face and his hat sailed into the dark. He spun and collapsed to the deck. There was a brief moment of spasm but then he lay motionless. Before the crew could react another tailed figure leapt from the water into the boat impacting the bald anchor man in the chest. He pummeled backward cracking his head off the boat's edge. The final member of the crew ran from the creature now lying in the boat. It had a mermaid's tail but of a larger size. There was long black hair flowing from its head but there were no mammary glands on the chest, instead sporting the translucent skin the female creatures had and faint, almost see-through, scales. The crewman ran from his first merman.

Racing into the wheelhouse, he grabbed the rifle before returning to the deck with it fully loaded. The merman was writhing on the floor attempting to haul himself along the deck. Watching him carefully, the crewman walked up slowly behind him. The merman managed to place a hand on the boats edge but was unable to haul himself over. His rifle raised, the crewman blew his shock, anger and vengeance through the merman's head, the boat's side and into the water. The fishing line, previously treasured, made its way out of the boat until it bucked hard caught around the wheelhouse. The line went tight several times before eventually becoming slack. Sitting down and curling himself up on the deck, the crewman never noticed.

Donald sat in the old, blue Astra and watched the car park closely. For five minutes he had seen no one but then a late night reveler had crossed the tarmac. Stumbling about in a drunken fashion, the man had come perilously close to the car before swerving away at the last minute to disappear at the far end of the car park. It would have been ironic, thought Donald, to get caught by some random lackey after avoiding those press bloodhounds.

The reporters from the nationals were more persistent than the local reporters who had more respect for the privacy of those involved in events. It had helped that Donald had grown up with some of the local ones and had promised them a fuller report in the morning. But the mainland hacks had remained and with it the prospect of missing the rendezvous at the pool to assess the mermaid's progress.

Time had marched on and they hadn't left and Donald felt pushed into extreme measures. An idea had come to him, brought to mind by some long forgotten gangster movie. It was mad but also so obvious it might work.

Kiera had a lot of photographic equipment and also the luggage to carry it. Immersed in her photography room, Donald was taken aback by the quality of her work. Not that he was an expert but it certainly seemed inventive and entertaining. Maybe he was biased though, after all he was deeply interested in the artist. Donald only hoped she would forgive his intrusion into her tools.

The trunk was quite large and seemed to hold stools and different boxes to make up shooting sets. "Portrait set-up" had been stamped on the side and as Donald unpacked, he found the contents beginning to fill the room, unable to recreate the configuration they had in the trunk. But the luggage was adequate, possibly roomy, the premise tested by Donald from inside. All that remained was to test the mermaid's co-operation.

He had gently coaxed the mermaid into looking at the box by throwing some fish into it. In a complicated mess of English and sign language, backed up with some "fish sounds", Donald explained his plan. The mermaid showed no comprehension or rebuke, preferring to stare at the fish in the trunk. Donald then tried to make a grab for the mermaid and to lift her but was treated to a loud shriek in his ear. With the reporters still outside, he dropped her instantly back into the bath. She went silent almost right away, much to his relief. This would be more difficult than anticipated.

With a roll of carpet tape behind his back, he sat next to the bath watching the mermaid feed. After feeding she was usually dopey and he now thought this would be the best chance to execute his plan. Watching her closely, he saw her eyes close. Quickly he slapped some tape across her mouth. She panicked and twisted, making the tape slip. Donald countered by taking the roll and wrapping it right round her head and mouth. Her hands thrust up to stop him but he was able to subdue them easily and tape them behind her back.

His mother had kept chickens and Donald remembered when they were moved it was the practice to keep them in the dark as this seemed to make them calmer. Quite how this applied to fish he wasn't sure but he forced the logic to make that jump and taped a towel over her eyes. With the blind in place, the mermaid did indeed calm down although he thought her body still showed a nervousness. Time to pack her up.

Looking back at this from the front seat of his car, Donald was amused at himself. He had forced the creature to be his captive without much remorse, believing it to be in her best interest. But lifting her into the trunk he had become uncomfortable, possibly embarrassed. Whilst not engaging in full sex, Kiera and Donald had become very intimate and he felt awkward at the mermaid's bare breasts. There was a strange betrayal to Kiera by even observing them and he felt compelled to throw a towel over her torso. As if in honour of Kiera, or maybe as a defence mechanism against thoughts about his captive, Donald took a moment to think about the evening ahead and of how Kiera would look when he arrived at the pool. A mix of hunger, pride, joy and excitement flowed through his mind and suddenly nothing could stop his task.

Lifting the mermaid, he gently placed her into the trunk, before setting padding around her. It was a tight fit but he wanted to prevent her from moving and hurting herself. Quickly, he closed the clasps on the trunk and turned the container onto its end. There was a brief rustle inside and then calm. Donald entered the living room and crossed to the window, peering out from the darkened space. They were still there and all his drive and excitement from dreaming of Kiera got destroyed. He needed help. That was when he decided to ring Kiera. With thoughts bouncing in his head about tapped phones, Donald decided to use his mobile and was relieved to see a single bar registering on the phone. At least something was in his favour. Usually it was a barely readable signal, useful for texting only.

When Kiera had spoken, he was picked up again. When Hayley sent the picture, Donald was pumped. After all the madness of the previous night, Donald felt like he was on a wild adventure again with this glorious beauty at his side. Now sitting in the car, he wondered was this just a man's hyped up thoughts or was this what life actually is before the sceptics drag you back down? He didn't know but she was glorious.

Getting the trunk into the boot had been ridiculously easy. This had been his main worry, that his plan would be incredibly obvious. When asked what was in the trunk, he had laughed that it was Kiera's and who can tell what a woman takes with her. Throwing a small rucksack into the boot afterwards, he had commented how little a man took along. The reporters had laughed. Well, except for the tall black haired woman. To be fair, it was an insult. And not one he would normally make.

Scanning the car park, Donald reached a decision. The mermaid had been in the trunk long enough and he needed to get this night moving. Calmly he got out of the car and approached the boot. Quickly, he gave a call to Kiera on her mobile. All was good. Donald opened the boot and found his knees starting to shake. Was it the mermaid, was it Kiera in her bikini, was it the whole crazy situation? Maybe it was this being the crux of it all, the first time they had shared their secret. Whatever, he was shaking.

With the strength given by adrenalin, he carried the trunk over to the front door without a hint of struggle. Hayley opened the door looking bemused at Donald's luggage. Despite his rush, Hayley's state of dress didn't escape Donald. A brief involuntary check of her was broken up by the sound of Kiera's voice. Donald was dumbstruck as Kiera came up to kiss his cheek and embrace him. It was strange how he had seen her wearing even less before but the location and situation made this even more erotic. If he could choose his dreams, this would be on the menu.

"What's in the case?" asked Hayley.

"One moment," answered Donald breathlessly and brushed past her carrying the case with Kiera racing behind him. Hayley followed them to the edge of the pool which was uncovered. From the far end, Tommy ran down the side. All lights were off but Tommy could see the bizarre trunk lying flat at the side of the pool.

"What's that?" he asked.

"Sorry guys but we had to get you here for this," said Donald and he unsnapped the clasps on the trunk.

"Bloody hell," gasped Hayley, looking at the tied up mermaid.

"Damn Donald, now that's kinky," marvelled Tommy.

# 15

# Private Pool

"That's a mermaid," said Hayley.

"Yes," said Donald, "and not a well one, which is why we need you." Hayley looked quizzically at Donald while Tommy just stared at the tied-up mermaid in the trunk.

"I know nothing about mermaids," protested Hayley.

"But you are a vet. You're kind of the expert as it goes," said Donald. Hayley started to shake her head. Kiera punched Donald's arm.

"Are you guys just going to stare at her or are we going to let her loose?"

"Loose! In my pool. No way Kiera, you must be joking. That's a public swimming pool," yelled Tommy.

"Flippin' heck Tommy, keep your voice down. You want us to get caught. Anyway you seemed happy enough with the idea of naked women in your pool twenty minutes ago," argued Kiera.

"Naked women?" said Donald.

"Hey, hang on Kiera," said Tommy, "nobody said nothing about a mermaid. I thought we were up to some late night loving here."

"She's not well?" interrupted Hayley, "what's up with her?"

"I don't know," said Donald, "we tried putting her back in the sea but she just can't swim."

"Back? How long have you had her?" asked Tommy.

"About a week," said Kiera. "Donald found her dying and brought her to my place. She's been in my bath since he rescued her." Kiera threw an admiring glance at Donald but it was lost on him as he petitioned Tommy for his catch.

"Come on Tommy, we need to get her in the water."

"I can't. Donald, I'll lose my job if anyone found out. Heck, I might even get nailed for us being in here."

"Please Tommy," begged Kiera, "She needs us. We've got nowhere to go from here. We need Hayley to take a look."

Tommy shook his head. "I'm sorry guys, but no. I can't." Tommy walked away holding his hands on his head and breathing heavily.

Kiera threw her arms around Donald and started to sniff, fighting back tears. Swearing under his breath, Donald stared at the mermaid, flummoxed.

"Give us a moment, Kiera," said Hayley, "I might just get some time to look at her. Let me talk to him. Just don't interfere." They watched Hayley follow Tommy towards the spa suite and shut the door behind her. The absurdity of the situation struck Donald, a passionate plea for the life of an, until now, mythical creature played out by protagonists in clothing better suited to a beauty contest. He laughed out loud.

"What on earth is funny about this?" asked Kiera.

"It'll be okay. Trust me."

"How do you know? How could you possibly know?"

"Cos' he'll do it for her. He doesn't stand a chance."

"Really and how do you work that out Sherlock? You don't even know them that well."

"One. We are here, so he really likes her. Two. She's wearing next to nothing. Three. She wants to help the mermaid. Four. He's about to get the snog he's been dying for since you guys arrived and then they'll walk back through, him holding her hand which she'll have placed firmly in his. For a date he'll do so much but for a girlfriend.... a potential mate."

"And how do you know that, my dear agony auntie?"

"Cos' I'd do it for you." Kiera beamed widely and without measure. Donald sure knew how to get under her skin. "Now are you going to help me cut her free?"

"Why's she tied up anyway?" asked Kiera.

"Would you let a strange man lock you away in a trunk?" Donald rolled his eyes at her, teasing.

"You're right Donald, look they're snogging."

"Hey, eyes down, give them some privacy and help me out."

Having been freed, the mermaid just lay in the trunk, seemingly in a state of shock from her travels. Together, Donald and Kiera lifted and gently dropped her into the water. The mermaid sank but started to move her arms and head about, scouting out the pool. Pulling off his track bottoms and top, Donald sat down on the poolside. He motioned for Kiera to sit beside him but she instead sat behind him and cuddled him tight. The heating had long been switched off and she was starting to feel a bit of a chill. Together they sat and watched as the mermaid began to move awkwardly under the water.

"She's incredible," said Hayley over their shoulder. Turning, Kiera saw Hayley stood hand in hand with Tommy, a picture of fascination filling her face. Tommy still looked pensive but was clearly trying to please Hayley.

"She is Hayley, she is," said Tommy. "Is she going to make the pool smell of like, fish or that? I mean, does she poo in there, or take a piss, cos I'm not sure that's going to be healthy?"

"Tommy, shush. Just look at her," chided Hayley.

"But Hayley, I have to think of people's health."

"Fish crap in the sea all the time and you eat from it and swim in it. Quite how she defecates I don't know but if someone has an accident in the pool you have ways of cleaning it. Kindly shut up and let me work." Oh, thought Donald, that hurt. Tommy's face dropped and he started to move slightly back. Spotting it and realising her enthusiasm for her role had pushed him away, she reached for his hands. Leading him back to the pool edge, she stood in front of him and then wrapped his arms round her placing them as high on her tummy as decency allowed. It was easy to forget the risk he was taking.

"Have you seen her swim at all?" asked Hayley.

"Never. She moves her tail at times but it seems laboured I think. Saying that I could be wrong. It's my first mermaid," said Donald.

"This won't be quick guys. I'll need to observe her. In truth, I don't even know if I can help. It's my first mermaid too."

"We open seven a.m. on Monday, Hayley," said Tommy, "You know we need to move her by then. They'll be no one here before that. You do what you need to." Hayley smiled and kissed him.

"You clever fox," Kiera whispered in Donald's ear. Turning his head, he kissed her neck before secretly replying,

"Hey, nakedness, and the promise of more nakedness. Don't blame me for understanding men."

"Are you all that easy?"

"For the right woman."

"And am I the right woman?"

"If you're asking that then you are one gorgeous, sexy, hot but ultimately, dense goddess."

She shoved him into the pool.

It was a quarter to five on Sunday morning and Kiera was feeling the cold. Hayley was in the pool examining the mermaid with Tommy's help. It had taken two hours of sitting poolside and feeding her fish before Hayley had gained the confidence of the mermaid. But Hayley's eyes had been on fire the whole time and Tommy was her willing accomplice.

Without any heating, out of the pool had become a cold place to sit especially when wet. At Hayley's request, Tommy had switched on the jacuzzi with its viewing window to the main pool and Kiera was taking full advantage of this new warmth.

"Do you think she's moving any better?"

Donald stepped up to the jacuzzi edge and grimaced. "I've no idea, Kiera. Hayley is very non-committal. Every time I ask a question it's like I'm in the way. Tommy's basically just taking orders and keeping stum. She's so focused."

"She's gotta get her better. There's no way we can hold on to her any longer," said Kiera.

"It was a good idea asking Hayley in on it. Tommy was touch and go but she seems to have him under her spell."

"Get in here."

Donald dropped into the water feeling the bubbles take the edge off the cold of his legs. Kiera slid across and lifted herself onto his lap. Her shoulders ached despite the water's attentions and Donald seemed to sense her need for a rub down as he started to work on her bare skin. It wasn't just the late night and now early morning but the whole passage of events over the last week that were finally coming to bear. Kiera could often be up and down with emotion but Donald was a mystery to her. Constantly, he would take things on as if they were nothing. Not devoid of emotion but rather a ship which despite being buffeted was able to hold an upright and straight course. Kiera was a careering tug tipped over taking on the monster waves.

Yet this morning she felt his weariness.

"What's up?"

"Well she's not exactly responding at any quick rate."

"Donald, it's only been a few hours. She's safe for the moment, let Hayley work her magic."

"I don't think there's magic to work Kiera."

"Donald, you've done more than others would. Take it easy." There was no answer. "What's really up?"

"Sorry. Oh, nothing, just a little tired." She turned round and straddled him as the jacuzzi switched off, bubbles fading to a stillness, the sound of the pump dying away. Taking his hands on her hips, she sat upright, letting him view her, staring deep into his eyes. The sullenness remained. There was something wrong.

"Tell me, Donald. Let me in. You can't carry it all." He stared her up and down before smiling.

"Damn you're beautiful." He held her hips, rubbing them gently. "Kiera, do you think ....... no, it's silly. Forget I asked."

"Tell me Donald."

"No, it's nothing."

Dammit, thought Kiera, open up to me. "Donald, tell me, or I'll punch you in the knackers." He laughed. Kiera breathed a sigh of relief. And then she waited. Two minutes passed.

"Kiera, is it the excitement that makes us feel like this? I mean it's surreal, all this madness, the mermaid, Alyssa the whole like exposure thing ..."

"You mean the inordinately amount of cleavage and boob talk the mermaids have generated and the close, exposed times you seem to find me in."

"Yeah, that."

"Maybe a bit, maybe."

"When it's all done will we still feel this rush, this hunger for each other?"

"I will. Donald, I will."

"I want to be around you. Want to be with you. Kiera, I want to..... love you..... I mean physically as well as like this."

"Good."

"But..."

"No buts."

"Hell, Kiera there are buts. There's always buts."

"Like what Donald? You rescued a half dead mermaid. Snuck her past the press in a suitcase. What exactly is the but in all this?"

"It'll be the questions, and the looks. Snide comments and things about you. Every time I'm over there with you, they'll be writing me off, taken in by you. Saying we're at it. Living in sin with the catholic girl."

"Who's they?"

"My Mum for one." Donald dipped his head. "She'll not like you. You're the wrong faith."

"Really. Or just not from here. Just not the conformist."

"Actually, you are the conformist," laughed Donald.

"Donald, do these things even matter? Am I not worth the risk?"

"I'm here, aren't I? I'm not saying you're not worth it. I'm just saying........ just sick of all the issues that go-around here. All the nonsense. The conformity. Why can't they just let people be people?"

"Donald, when I arrived here they asked me all about me. They wanted to know everything but do you know what, they told me next to nothing about themselves. Because they are afraid. Afraid of what everyone else thinks. What people will say. It's all a house of cards Donald. Running round propping up the sides, making sure people can't see what's underneath."

"And you think I have my own house of cards."

"It comes with growing up here. But you are trying to break out. You carried a half-naked mermaid up to my place, rescued a topless model, and are now cavorting with a catholic girl and her mate on the Sabbath in a swimming pool. You're beyond scandal, Donald. But you did it all because you care about people, about creatures."

"Kiera, you're ...."

"Shush, just enjoy this moment. We won't get this jacuzzi to ourselves like this again." Kiera move closer and brushed intimately with Donald.

"Kiera, Tommy might see."

"I think Hayley is plenty enough woman for him." The bubbles started again.

# 16

# Ignition

The traffic was extremely busy for a Sunday morning. Of course, one would expect to see the church going populace but on a grim day such as the morning was turning out to be, anyone else would surely be in their bed. Even the dog walkers would have second thoughts.

The peppering of droplets of water, with just the hint of ice before it melted, attacked the windscreen of Tommy's car forcing him to move the wipers from intermittent to a constant to and fro. Grey dominated the skyline but within that base lurked the torrid cumulonimbus clouds that caused the hail and sleet. The weather changed fast on the island, due to swirling southerly winds that dominated, dragging inclement weather from the mainland. Tommy thought of the cold but clear winters that could come with a high pressure forcing a northerly or even easterly wind. Often, they were so much better than the summers.

Glancing at his rear view mirror, he caught a glimpse of Kiera's bag. Ready lined with a large, black bin bag, the tweed carrier could take a reasonable weight similar to a moderate holdall. Although Donald had brought a significant quantity of fish with him, he had also left some in Kiera's freezer, worried that the smell of defrosting fish would give a not so subtle perfume in the changing areas. So Tommy had been sent out on a run to fetch these. Now that she had had time to study the mermaid, Hayley had a few ideas about some drugs that could help it. The technicalities were a mystery to Tommy but her presence in the car was more than enjoyable.

His back was sore from spending most of the night assisting his veterinary companion and he was positively wrinkled from long term exposure to the water. Still the image of Hayley in her bikini was not leaving his mind in a hurry. He glanced sideways. Like she needed to be wearing a bikini. Damn, he thought, how did I ever get the eyes off this one? Despite being well liked by most people, Tommy had often found women hard to relate to. Yet Hayley's fun attitude combined with her dedication to her work had made him risk a wild night. Just how mad or confusing a night he hadn't expected.

"Lot of cars about for Sunday," said Tommy.

"Yeah. Yes, there is."

"You okay, you seem miles away at the moment."

"It's okay Tommy. I'm just wrecked. Up all night and trying to focus, I can barely see straight."

"Just make sure you pick up the right drugs," laughed Tommy pulling into the veterinary car park. Hayley opened the door and rocked towards it before rolling back and turning to Tommy.

"Thank you."

"Thank me? Why?"

"Last night. You were expecting something else but it didn't turn out the way you hoped."

"No, but I don't think you expected to see a fish woman

either."

"No, but thank you. You let me get on with it. All night, you just were there, helping. Thank you. I didn't know you had a heart for animals."

"Hayley, look animals are fine but last night I stood in that water for one reason. You. It looked important to you, you were obviously in the zone with it. So I thought she wants to do this, I have to help her. Didn't seem the time to be demanding anything else."

"Oh, demanding is it?"

"Hey, whoa. Sorry. I meant looking. No, asking. Hoping."

Hayley laughed out loud before swinging back to the door. Starting to open it, she had a second thought and swung back to Tommy. Reaching her hands forward she brought their mouths to touch before exploring. His wide eyed surprise saw her eyes close before he shut his own eyes too. He felt her hands take his and a shudder went up his body as she placed them where only lovers are allowed. Despite the clothing, his delight was palatable as she broke off the kiss. Savouring a few last moments, his hands finally fell.

"Well that woke me up." Embarrassed, Tommy could only smile. "I'll go get the gear," said Hayley. "Least I know you won't leave while I'm gone." With several glances back to the car, Hayley made her way through the cold rain into the practice. Sat behind the wheel, Tommy was oblivious to the various vehicles with satellite dishes making their way along the road, towards the harbour front. Even the return of Hayley startled him.

"Got them. Think I can pretend they're for a friend's aquarium although the dosage is going to be a mystery. Better make out there was some sort of epidemic." Tommy just smiled, still lost in the previous moment. "Tommy, you there."

"Yeah, sorry. Just tired."

"Yeah right. Guess I'd be annoyed if you hadn't enjoyed it." Tommy blushed. "To Kiera's then."

Pulling out of the practice drive, Tommy found himself stuck in a long queue. It was becoming clearer that some people were bypassing the traffic on the footpaths and several cars were just parked up on the pavement.

"What the hell's all this?" Tommy said out loud to himself. About a minute later the cars had come to a complete halt, much to the anger of several news crews trying to get to the front of the excitement. A large gentleman in a suit with gaudy tie swore loudly at an elderly lady who seemed to be frozen in her car, frightened by the level of traffic. Opening the lady's door, he gave a diatribe of abuse. That's not right, thought Tommy.

Gazing at the obnoxious man, it took Hayley a moment to realise Tommy had exited the car. By the time she had got out herself, Tommy was shouting at the man. Hayley was never sure of the exact words that caused Tommy's reaction but the phrase "stupid effing bitch" was definitely in there. Within seconds of the words being spoken, Tommy had delivered a right hook, connecting with the man's jaw and flooring him. A man with a camera grabbed the suited man by the collar calling "come on". Rising, the man vowed he would have sued Tommy if it hadn't have been for the bodies ahead.

Watching the man scarper, Tommy was aware of Hayley grabbing his shoulder squeezing hard against his torso but Tommy was more intent on the car's occupant. He extended a hand and the lady climbed out of the vehicle.

"Thomas Clarke, always said you would amount to nothing. What are doing going round hitting people like that?" Hayley watched Tommy stand upright, head dropped ashamed.

"Just a minute, lady. My Tommy just stepped in for you, sorted that guy who was giving you a lip-full. Think you owe him some thanks." The old lady was laughing, garbed in her black Sunday dress under a dull coat with a dowdy hat covering pinned up hair. She smiled at Hayley's response.

"Got a woman too. You might do yet Thomas Clarke. Defender of the weak. Now off with you, I won't make church dallying like this. A good Godly stroll is required." With that she toddled off not once looking back.

"Bloody cheek, Tommy. And after you helping her. And your hand. The knuckles, are they bleeding?"

"My Tommy. My Tommy. I Iike it Hayley. Babe, I love it."

"Who was that, anyway, daft old bat?"

"That was no daft old bat. That was Mrs Macleod, picked me up from a rascal and got me where I am today. Right battleaxe but she did me a lot of good. Arrogant bugger picking on her."

"Where was he going anyway Tommy?"

"Said something about bodies. But hey, we got your patient to get back to anyhow. We'll have to turn round and go to Kiera's via the back road, there's no going through town with this traffic."

"If you want to have a look we can. She'll be okay for twenty more minutes. It's not like she's going anywhere. Anyway a stroll with my Tommy wouldn't go amiss." Hayley grabbed his hand and they wandered down the street to the harbour front abandoning the car like everyone else.

There was an immense crowd around the number three pier, all eyes seemingly concentrated on a small fishing boat, tied to the side with policemen on board. A young sailor was giving a statement and there was dark, brownish blood on the boat deck. A dull murmuring of the crowd was broken by occasional yells and heated arguments and the general argy-bargy of interested onlookers. Various reporters were milling about interviewing locals and sight-seers alike, grabbing whatever take they could on the tale of the boat.

"Heck Tommy, what's all this about? Look at that boat, the blood on it."

"Looks like a drunken brawl or something on board. You don't think someone's been murdered do you."

"Not from losing that blood Tommy, that's not human blood."

"Hayley, look over there at those placards. Save the mermaids!"

"You think there's been more?"

Tommy pulled Hayley close like he was about to kiss her but whispered in her ear. "Careful. You don't know who's listening in a crowd like this." Hayley nodded as they moved apart. "Anyway Hayley, look there's Seamus on duty, he'll know."

Keeping a watchful eye at the back of the crowd was the town's traffic warden. With nothing moving in the main street, he was taking a restful moment leaning up against the oldest town pub with its dirty wash walls and dark musty windows.

"Still here from last night then?" laughed Tommy.

"Clarkie, you rascal. How's it going? Hope you're not messed up in this business."

"Just out with my wee woman here. Seamus, you remember Hayley from school." Seamus looked blank. "Two years below us."

"Sorry love but no. My loss mind, my loss. Surely you can do better than this Hayley," joked Seamus. Hayley giggled and then grabbed Tommy's arm pulling him close.

"So what's the craic, Seamus?"

"Haven't you heard? Well obviously not otherwise you wouldn't be asking. Tommy, you know all this mermaid talk, well, it seems it's true."

Tommy tried to seem surprised. "You're having a laugh."

"No, no bull today. There's a dead one on that boat. Well a dead merman to be exact."

"How did that happen?" asked Hayley feeling a rush of tears. She detested animals dying, especially violently.

"That boat belongs to old Macreedie. He's up in the hospital on life support. Apparently, he got hit by the merman at some point. Another of his crew was also attacked and has severe concussion, being kept under observation. The young lad blew the brains out of the merman apparently." Hayley buried her head into Tommy on hearing the detail.

"So why were they attacked?" asked Tommy.

"Well the young lad, I heard from Smith the CID guy when I was grabbing a coffee for him, was keeping pretty stum but they believe Macreedie may have had a mermaid on the line."

"Bloody hell Seamus. Have there been a lot seen?"

"Not that I know of Tommy but seems like they are out there. Seems Fish-Tales may not be as mad as we thought." Hayley raised her eyes at Tommy.

"Iain, who shot that boobs-out model. Used to get called Fish-tales at school."

"God, what's the commotion behind there?" The couple turned to where Seamus was looking and saw an ambulance forcing its way down the street. "Sorry guys, gotta go."

"Hell, Tommy, we need to tell Kiera and Donald. This changes things."

Tommy held her arms gently. "No we don't, not right away. Nothing changes. We get things sorted at the pool and then early hours tomorrow we release her down the shore. She swims off and that's it. Back to nature, taking a chance with all the other fish."

"But Tommy," forced Hayley in a whispered hush, "She's not like the other fish. She's ......."

"Human?"

Hayley nodded.

"Hayley, you're a vet. Think about it. They just look a bit like us. You even recognised the blood difference from fifty yards away."

"But they're like us. Just with tails."

"No Hayley, no. Just stop. They smell of fish, they certainly don't crap like us and they don't talk like us."

"But they look so human."

"Yes, look. But they're not. As much as that rack on the mermaid perks up my interest, she sure isn't human. Dammit Hayley, I wouldn't go to bed with one."

"And this is your salient test of humanness?"

"Hey, don't dis a man's libido."

"So what, it's just a fish?"

"That's unfair babe. I didn't say they were worth nothing, just they weren't human."

"Let's just go Tommy. Can't believe they killed it. They're beautiful."

Placing an arm around Hayley, Tommy led her back towards the car, his head flicking once at some resounding cheers. A body was being lifted up off the boat and had become visible to the crowd. There was cheering and booing before the gathering began to push and shove. Turning his back and keeping this from Hayley, Tommy missed the start of the biggest brawl the island had seen that year, even surpassing the New Year's Eve early closing disaster at the Trawlerman's pub.

# 17

# Riot

"Well, I believe the council, or the government, maybe military, someone needs to go after and eliminate these beasts before another poor sailor gets taken out by them. These creatures aren't natural and need stopping."

The journalist nodded her head sagely as the man spoke into the camera. All along the harbour front the crowds were pushing for a view of the doomed boat and its tell-tale blood stain. Discussion was ripe about just how blood-thirsty the arrivals were and animal rights groups had formed their own picket line near the boat. The island's police force was stretched and had pulled in all reserves in order to cover this latest situation. In a place where the regular weekly excitement amounted to domestic disturbances, drunken brawls or the occasional happy Saturday night flasher, recent events were showing a darker side to the advertised ideal of peace and beauty.

Preaching on "God's creation" that morning Reverend Murdo McKinney had felt an uneasy aura around his congregation. Several comments at the door beyond the usual "thank you minister, that was lovely", gave him cause for concern that he had offended a few of the quieter elements of his flock. Some of the elders were definitely offended but there was nothing new there. On returning home, he had heard the news on the radio and had decided to make for the town to assess what was really happening. Now in the midst of the throng, he felt uneasy to the core.

"Reverend McKinney, a word, minister." Blast, thought the minister, not now.

"Minister, are you here to condemn these hellish creatures and send them back to the pits they come from? Minister, there's media people here looking for interviews. You should get hold of one and show them our church is pushing God's word to the front and condemning these hateful things. After your unclear message this morning this will have the people behind you. I can guarantee the kirk session will be supporting you all the way."

Iain Maciver, thought Murdo, always to the fore telling me what to say, to think. I bet there's at least three others with him. Turning, Murdo saw he was under-estimating. Seven elders greeted his gaze. Ah, this must be serious. At least three of them are hardly ever seen within the church at all except for the "Show-times". Clowns like these could whip this up into something seriously dangerous and not just for the mermaids.

"Well minister, will you be talking to them?"

"Iain Maciver, understand this. I will seek to understand this situation and then, only if necessary, shall I comment on it. And if I do, it will not be for the benefit of our church, denomination or island. Instead it will be only for those it is intended for. As for your backing, I'd feel greater protection standing on the Machair in a force ten. Now if you have nothing of use to say then kindly give my ears some rest. Have a blessed afternoon and try not to fret on too many more schemes to oust me!"

Indignation seemed contagious as it spread from Iain MacIver's face to those of the other elders like the sweep of a paintbrush. Fighting for the cutting response, Maciver flapped briefly before delivering only a curt "minister" before turning on his heel to be followed by his party. Well Laura would be delighted, thought Murdo. And God help me find what words are needed in all this.

His train of concentration was broken by a tap on the shoulder. Ninety-four year old Mr McCauley, erstwhile elder of Murdo's congregation and the foremost member in standing up to any change in "the way things are done" stared into the eyes of his minister. Disagreeing with Murdo on a weekly basis about style and furniture within the church, McCauley had been a fixture in the community all his life. Murdo felt another bashing was on the way.

"Reverend McKinney, you do well to put a lid on Maciver. A time for wise and calm heads. Remember "for such a time as this". This may be your time, Esther."

And with that he was gone. Not in a flash but with a determined, if staggered, walk into the crowd. And there's nothing new under the sun Lord, thought Murdo? Well I never saw that one coming. Feeling buoyed by this development, Murdo strode towards the boat to see first-hand the tale of woe.

Finding a small gap, Murdo stood staring at the scene trying to imagine what had happened. The obvious blood stain sent a shiver down his back. Coupled with the discontent in the crowd, he could feel his body tense. Debates between elements of the crowd seemed to be increasing and cursing and accusations began to fly. Murdo soaked in the whole scene and then quietly closed his eyes, offering silent prayers to his God. Prayers for calm, for healing and for the demons not to take hold of the raw emotions stirred.

The crowd suddenly squashed tighter together as a police car pulled up and Murdo saw the local Chief Inspector dodge questions, before heading past the police cordon at the boat and disappearing into the bland tent on the quayside where evidence had been taken. A hunger for the reason for this development struck the onlookers and all kinds of wild theories started to circulate.

"They know they're killers. They know. But they're going to protect them. We need to cull them from our shores." The speaker was a normally unpopular councillor that Murdo recognised. "And they mean to stand and keep our shores and fishermen from being safe." The councillor was pointing at a teenage girl standing with a group of students holding animal rights banners. Behind her rounded glasses, she wore a face of utter defiance.

"We don't hunt lions or snakes. We don't own this world, it's for every animal." Being quite small didn't stop the girl from being heard, as her powerful voice cut through the crowd. "You're just scared of what you don't understand." Last week, thought Murdo, it was all about indecency, how exposed they were. Now it's about killing.

"All this time they've been there. They've killed a man before. McClaren was right. Took his bloody Dad to the depths. They need eradicating."

"How dare you! These are beautiful, intelligent creatures, doing less harm to this planet than you with your supermarkets and your television. Bloody power stations causing famine across the world and freak storms. You're as much a killer as any mermaid!"

The bickering continued and became a full blown row. Murdo felt helpless to intervene, not blessed with a loud voice himself. Trying time and again to think of the right calming words, his brain came up empty and the verbal temperature about him rose higher. And then he heard the whispers. At first, barely audible below the raging words, it began to grow until both debaters started to find out what the commotion was. Across at the harbour, Murdo watched a policeman call into his microphone handset and several officers were suddenly trying to break through the crowd from the wrong side towards the evidence tent.

The animal rights girl had started to shout again about the evil done to animals by men when the councillor leapt onto a wall and faced the crowd. Rage was on his face and his fist was raised in anger.

"It's killed the Captain. He's dead. The hospital say he's dead. Our fisherman is dead, killed by the mermaids. They're killers. Killers, killers, killers....." The chant grew until the noise was deafening. Murdo was reminded of his early days as a minister when a man in the local community was suspected of being a paedophile and of the rage of the mob around him as he failed to calm people down. It's time to act, he thought. Get this young girl out of here and let them chant themselves out. With the anger at the news, there'll be no reasoning at the moment. Stepping towards the girl, he was dismayed to see her being lifted by her associates above crowd level.

"You're the killers. You're the dumb animal destroying the world. You stupid, dense bastard. Bloody retard."

"Who you calling a retard, you bitch? Get them!"

Murdo was caught in the surge and saw the girl topple off the shoulders of her supporters, crashing onto her back, her head smacking the pavement below. Her allies scattered, some getting a punch or a kick for their efforts. But the girl received a hard kick from a large man who was swearing at her. Murdo realised he couldn't stop the man and so dived on top of the girl. First a stamp on the back. Then a kick to the ribs. Then a blow just behind his ear. Then just a blur of pain with parts of his body taking turns to yell out the loudest. Then the cries of a policeman. Then just black.

It had only been six months as a full constable and the fear welled up inside Chrissy as she saw the charge. Instinct, or maybe good training had caused her to jump onto the wall when she saw the girl topple and she managed to bypass the retreating animal rights crowd. Getting to the minister who had dived onto the girl wasn't easy but Chrissy had her night stick drawn and pepper spray ready as she leapt into the fray.

Striking the knees and with the element of surprise, she cleared a path and stood over the minister. Ideally, she should have shouted a warning and told everyone to stand down but the boots were still flying and fists being swung. Copiously, but with aimed intent, she pepper sprayed those closest before striking down the few who didn't turn away. There was brief retreat of the tide and she estimated she had maybe ten seconds to get the girl, the minister and herself clear. Looking down, she saw he was bleeding from the head and probably unconscious. Hell, thought Chrissy, this isn't going to work.

She looked up into the face of a small man, seeing a wailing banshee. From the corner of her eye, a right hook was appearing and she tilted back but was caught hard on the shoulder. The blow forced her to her knees. She anticipated the next blow but was caught unaware as it failed to land. Looking up, the man was flat on his back and Sergeant DJ Macleod was racing down with his hands. Rolling the man, he slammed his foot onto the man's back, pinning him to the floor. The immediate crowd drew back, stunned. The rebuke of "anyone else?" failed to get a response.

Inside the evidence tent, the forensic expert was leaning over the merman's body when the front door burst open and the mob screamed at him for it. His cries of "it's dead" went unheeded and he was knocked aside, tumbling out the side entrance barely managing to hold onto the pier edge and stop himself from dropping into the sea. When he regained his composure he saw the creature's body being carried above the masses, like a morbid form of rock star, crowd surfing. His police colleagues looked battered and were in disarray, far too few in number to cope with the savage outburst.

# 18

# Crisis

Donald looked into the office of the leisure center and saw Tommy and Hayley asleep on a blow-up mattress. With an arm hooked around her, his face was buried in the mass of hair at her neck. Everything was quiet except for a low electrical hum. They look happy, he thought. Which was something considering the news they had brought back, that other mermaids had been found. The tension amongst the group had heightened and they knew they needed to move the mermaid that night. It was not a good idea to be found concealing such a creature during this maelstrom of opinion.

It had been decided that all of the group would be needing some sleep and Tommy had dug out the old blow-up from the depths of a storage cupboard. After hunting for a pump of some variety, Tommy had returned with a hand-held and proceeded with the inflation. The bed turned out to be larger than he thought and it completely filled the office such that part of it was under the side wall table. With the aid of some blankets and towels, the accommodations were complete and Donald suggested the girls take the first nap time. Kiera had refused and told the other couple to catch forty winks as they had been the busier. Sometimes Kiera's thoughtful nature had its downsides.

She was still at the poolside watching the mermaid, trying to assess if Hayley's drugs were having an effect. Needing some air, Donald had popped outside briefly before returning past the office. Tommy hadn't increased the heating in the building in case it was noted in costs and Donald felt a little cold. A coffee should help, he thought and made for the machine by the café.

Dropping some coins in, Donald waited patiently for his brew. The coffee machine was a modern one and the drink was made from real beans. While this was preferable, it meant a longer waiting time. The café had a long set of windows beside it from where you could view the pool and his eyes were attracted to the dark-haired girl with her legs dangling in.

He could always see the train coming through the tunnel, that was his problem. Everything in some shape or other always came crashing down. Once there was dreams of living and working on the mainland but his qualifications hadn't been good enough and then his mum had that little bout of illness. With no one else to take care of her, Donald had had to do his duty. So often things had never materialised into something special. He couldn't let that happen with Kiera. Only the beep of completion from the machine brought him back from staring at her.

Sipping his coffee, he nearly burnt his lips and caused a slight spillage with his reactions. Grabbing a napkin he wiped the mess, remembering that their presence here should be kept under wraps. Strange, in the building it was like the world was far away, he thought. A little island of their own, peace to help the mermaid, calm to get closer to each other. There seemed to be oneness of purpose with the four of them. No, make it five, after all the mermaid was in on this. Here, right now, he was actually content. If this was all there was to life, it might actually be enough. A purpose and Kiera. Lord, he thought, we really are such simple creatures.

Holding his cup to the window, Donald knocked it with his free hand, then indicating as to whether she wanted coffee. She nodded and held up two fingers to indicate how long she would be. Turning away, he noticed the television on the wall. Reaching up, he pushed the power button but was only able to make a single red light come on at the base of the television. Scanning, Donald couldn't see any remote controls lying about and so began looking for further switches on the television. Seeing some he pressed until the screen sprang into life.

It was one of the all-day news channels. Apparently City had enjoyed a solid win over United. Donald wasn't a football fan of any note and turned away. His eye was caught by the approaching Kiera, still in her bikini but with a towel draped over her shoulders. Her coffee, whoops, he thought.

"I'm just getting your coffee now."

"Did you forget? Tell me you didn't forget me from there to here. Was it that goggle-box there that did it?"

"No, no. I was just a bit pre-occupied." She stepped forward throwing her arms around Donald, dropping the towel in the process and then engaged his lips with her own. Her right leg slid round his left, hooking onto it tight. For a long moment she held this pose before breaking off slowly.

"So you'll remember me better." Donald stood dumb-founded by this show of affection. Kiera's frequent but forward expressions of love were still causing him to be uncomfortable but he didn't want them to stop. He stood and looked at her body. Drinking in her white flesh, her wet, sticky hair and her bikini cleavage, he was aware he was like a puppy with its tongue out, lapping. Still she didn't seem to mind.

"Coffee? Any chance, lover?"

Donald dropped more coins in the machine and Kiera took a seat at one of the plastic chairs of the café. The café itself was basic with its garden furniture tables and chairs and sachets of sauces in small plastic baskets on each table.

"No sound on the telly then?"

"No, Kiera, can't find the remote."

"Not to worry, they have those subtitles on."

The screen showed a chemical plant in a hot country. Large plumes of smoke were pouring out from a raging fire and several vehicles were surrounding it. Although they looked primitive, the red colour indicated these were indeed fire tenders.

Kiera turned back to face Donald as he placed a coffee in front of her. Sitting down opposite her, his face looked as if it was pondering something before he suddenly sat forward.

"Why don't you get that gorgeous figure over here?"

"Oh, are you becoming a bit demanding?" Kiera giggled. "Telling your girl what's what?"

"Haul that horny body my way. Time for some Donnie loving."

Kiera never moved. Instead a look of horror shot across her face and she looked right past Donald. Damn, thought Donald, that's not gone down well.

"Sorry Kiera, I just thought..."

"Donald, shut up." Bloody hell, thought Donald, I've really done it.

"Kiera, it was only a joke. Well a not a joke, I did want you round here for ....... you know.... and I ..."

"Donald, will you shut up please and look, just look." Kiera was pointing at the television.

There was a fishing boat on the screen with some blood on the deck. The colour of the blood was a little strange. There were pictures of several fishermen and as Kiera scanned the text appearing as subtitles she saw the words "now confirmed dead." Swallowing hard, she reached out for Donald's hand but he was too engrossed to see this. Then there was a montage of film of a riot where she could see Reverend Murdo McKinney fall to the ground. The words "may find this footage distressing" was accompanied by still pictures showing a merman being carried aloft though he seemed rather bloodied.

"Donald, what are we going to do? Look at them, baying for blood." Donald never looked round but instead stood up and approached the television as if the distance was preventing him from seeing properly. There was now a particular still in the background while the newsreader continued behind a modern desk complete with laptop. Donald suddenly turned round.

"There! Falling to the floor. Actually more like diving. That's Murdo."

"What are we going to do? Heck, Donald, the news says there's a state of emergency. Police telling everyone to stay indoors. Donald, what do we do?"

"Take it easy, Kiera, we've got time. Not a lot but we have time. Get Tommy and Hayley up 'cos we need to talk about this." Donald turned away towards the front door.

"Where are you going?"

"I'm going to go outside and phone Laura, see how Murdo

is. That looked bad. Then we are going to get out of here."

Kiera walked the short distance to the office, her heart pounding. The excitement of discovery of a mermaid, of her blossoming relationship with Donald, of the fun of hiding out in the leisure center was paling. Once again there seemed to be a dark side to the mermaid's arrival, even if it wasn't their fault.

She stopped briefly outside the door, drawing a calming breath and then opened the door with purpose. After a quick glance, she exited the office with the word "sorry" repeated several times. Whilst she enjoyed intimate moments of a physical nature herself, she was never one to enjoy observing it in others. Safely outside, she faced away from the door and announced Donald's decision that a meeting was required right now.

After a brief pause when she considered waiting, Kiera decided the better course was to make her way back to the café. After all, the couple would soon find their way there. Donald was still outside, so she took her coffee and stood at the window watching the mermaid. "The mermaid" just didn't sound right. She needed a name. Almost as if her mind was trying to step away from the horror of the incidents surrounding the creature, the name just came to her. Tink. Little Tink. Our own little piece of fairytale. And if we don't look after her, then she's going to die.

A tap on the shoulder brought her back. She hadn't heard his footsteps, too engrossed in her thoughts but she felt his arms slide round her waist to hold her tight. Leaning back into him, she allowed herself a moment of pleasure, of comfort, of finding strength.

"What the hell's the crisis? We were in a moment there,

Kiera. In fact we nearly had reached THE moment," said Tommy.

"Sorry guys," apologised Kiera.

"What's up?" asked Hayley seeing Kiera's worried face.

"It's the mermaid," replied Donald.

"Tink."

"What, Kiera?" queried Donald.

"I've called her Tink. Seems right."

"That's lovely," agreed Hayley and digging Tommy in the ribs as he rolled his eyes.

"Okay then, Tink," said Donald. "Well Tink and ourselves have a problem. Apparently McCreedie is dead. All hell's broken loose in town and they were carrying a merman through the streets. Cut it right up." Hayley began to weep. Placing a hand on her shoulder, Tommy looked at Tink.

"How bad is it out there?" he asked Donald.

"Well, Reverend McKinney was injured and I just spoke to his wife. He's in a bad way in the hospital."

"The news said there's a state of emergency," interjected Kiera.

"Well that's wrong, Kiera. Laura said that there's all our police about and they are telling everyone to stay indoors but there's no emergency. She did say things were heated though. There's been a few more clashes between animal rights people, camera crews and the public. Everyone's talking, taking sides. This would not be a good time to be found with a mermaid in our care."

"No," agreed Tommy, "Is she fit, Hayley? Will she be okay to move tonight?"

"I don't know Tommy. I'll be able to tell you in a few hours."

"We need to go now," said Donald, "When I spoke to Laura,

she said that the leisure center was going to be used for a press conference tonight. I expect you'll get a phone call soon Tommy."

"A press conference?" queried Tommy.

"Yes, to take things away from the sea front, they reckon the town hall's too close. So we need to move now and you need to get this place back to normal, Tommy."

"We can't take Tink now," protested Hayley, "I'm not sure she's okay to be going out there."

"Then we need to find somewhere to put her. And I'm guessing a bath tub's no longer suitable." Hayley shook her head. "Right guys, let's get dressed and moving, we ain't got much time."

"Donald, wait I've had a text. Apparently they want to be here at five. What's that give us? Two hours?"

"Okay, Tommy," said Donald, "you stay here with Kiera and get this place sorted. Hayley and me will take Tink out of here and we'll text you when we get somewhere suitable. Agreed?" Tommy nodded and Hayley grabbed him and gave a strong but brief kiss. Motioning at Donald to follow, she made for the pool. Kiera held Donald's hand and looked into his eyes sensing the fear inside.

"You got this. Go on, sort it out. Love you." She was taken by surprise at his rapid embrace and the deepness of his kiss. But then he was gone, following Hayley. She looked at Tommy and smiled.

"Okay, what's first?"

"Well I'll be a gent. You sort out the café and the office, then get onto the changing rooms."

"What are you going to do?"

"I'm taking the crap out of the pool but if you want it the

job's yours!"

# 19

# A New Man on the Scene

Reverend Murdo McKinney opened his eyes and believed he could finally see the trees clapping their hands. A moment's squinting brought his view into true focus and a welcome face smiled warmly at him.

"How's Iron Man?"

"Laura, what.... where am I?" asked Murdo. As the question left his mouth, he could smell the disinfectant and feel the courser white sheets covering his body. His backside touching the bed sheet also made him think of those open backed gowns.

"Hospital, dear. You took quite a kicking. Had me worried."

"Sorry, but they were almost on her."

"You were very brave. I expect no less from you. But you really did get thumped."

Murdo tried to sit up but his ribs stabbed at him, giving a searing pain until he lay back again. He noticed some tubes in his arm and a metal stand holding a clear liquid in a bag. His head pounded and everything had a general ache.

"Two broken ribs, Murds. Severe bruising all over. You also had some bleeding from your head but turned out not to have been anything to do with the brain. Least that's what they said to me."

"But how's the girl?"

"Little shaken, a few bruises from the odd kick you didn't get in the way of, but fine. Haven't seen her since they discharged her. Thought she might have dropped by."

"At least she's okay. That's what matters."

"Yes but a thankyou doesn't go amiss," answered Laura, puffin herself up in indignation like an angry ward sister. They sat in silence for a while, looking out the window to the miserable, grey sky.

"There was a meeting last night too. Sounded pretty rough." Laura described the news report she had heard that morning. Trying hard to focus, Murdo struggled to believe how violent reactions had been.

"This will end in more deaths if they don't stop these mob antics. Whipping people up against mere animals. I should get out there and …."

"Like the blazes, Murdo McKinney, you will sit on your backside and work at getting better. Nothing else. You're on a time-out mister." Murdo murmured a response but then feel silent to his wife's obviously better judgement. Only the occasional trolley being wheeled up and down in the corridor outside was heard, allowing the couple to enjoy their peace together.

"Oh, good news. Alyssa had her operation and she's doing well. Transferring up here, anytime really. James is seeing to her, he's quite smitten. I said she could stay at ours. After all, you're going to be here for a day or two so I can get on with looking after proper invalids." Laura gave a wry smile as Murdo cast a sullen look in her direction.

The morning air blew across Kiera's face as she sat beside the storm kettle waiting for the water to boil. Huddled up in Donald's coat, she watched her man wash himself in the sea water. Dipping his head in fully, he then stood up and she saw little rivulets run down his back before he mopped them up with a towel. She was so engrossed that she never heard the kettle boil but reacted instead to the fluid spitting out of the stumpy spout.

"Hey, Donald, hurry up, coffee's ready. Shout them two as well."

Donald had brought some meagre supplies with him, croissants and scones and a jar of coffee. Hayley was unable to wait until after breakfast and had ventured into the loch with Tommy to see if Tink was alright. After an explanation of how Donald had found her naked in the sea, Hayley had decided she now required some clothing when she swam and took a t-shirt of Donald's with a promise to pick up her swimsuit soon as. Clearly she was all about Tommy, so Kiera wondered why she felt threatened by Hayley being seen in the raw by Donald, especially as all it had achieved was a great deal of embarrassment. Damn, we are funny, she thought.

Tommy was keen to show off his figure and had swam in his boxers which pleased Hayley greatly. Kiera insisted that to save further embarrassment they should exit the water just down a little bit where she would leave their clothing. Towels were another forgotten necessity. Donald sat down to his coffee placing a protective arm around Kiera's back. Mine, she thought, all mine.

"She seems a lot friskier," announced a fully clothed Hayley, grabbing at a croissant and devouring it hungrily.

"Just like Hayley," laughed Tommy, who got a stuck-out

tongue as a reply.

"How long, Hayley?" asked Donald.

"How long what?"

"Until she's good to go back. Until she no longer needs babysitting."

"Not sure, as long as it takes. Why, do you need to go?"

"No, it's just with all this hassle I want her far away, and us not in the middle of it."

The foursome quietly ate their breakfast, tiredness seeping into their bodies. Tommy was conscious of attending to the leisure center, knowing the damage that needed to be assessed. Kiera and Donald were both free while Hayley needed to drop by the practice although she doubted it would be open considering the recent events. Taking a short walk to his car, Tommy returned announcing the schools were closed and that the police, due to the recent riots, had asked everyone to stay at home in order to avoid any repeat and for tempers to calm down. Hayley agreed to go to the center with Tommy but first she wanted to check on Tink.

Kiera watched Hayley walk along the shoreline scanning into the sea. At regular intervals she would shake her head and start staring afresh into a different sector of the loch. Tommy was hailed over and sent out in the opposite direction. After an hour, as Kiera was tidying up the camp, Hayley came back looking very anxious.

"There's no sign of her. No sign at all. I don't think she's here."

"That's a good thing, isn't it Hayley?" asked Kiera.

"No, it's not. She was no way fit enough to be swimming back out into the sea. She was still struggling when we saw her earlier. Wounded animals never last long."

"Nothing Hayley," said a breathless Tommy on his return, "I've checked it all along, just nothing."

"Well, she must have gone back out to sea," surmised Donald.

"No. No, no, no. That's not it, Donald. Take my word, that's not it."

"But it makes sense, Hayley," countered Kiera, "she's gone home."

"Trust me she hasn't. I can feel it. Tommy, listen to me. She hasn't."

"Okay, take it easy," said Donald, "what do you suggest?"

"We need to follow the loch edges and then check out those little lochs that this one feeds. Even the really small ones. Some of them have a depth to them that could be suitable, I think. Look, some of this I'm having to guess at because at the end of the day, Tink's a mermaid. But something isn't right, trust me."

"Okay," agreed Donald, watching Tommy wrap his arms around Hayley, "we brought you into this so it's the least we can do to listen to you."

They decided to separate into two groups, Tommy and Hayley going east, Donald and Kiera moving west. Donald watched the couple depart as Kiera packed away the last of the basic camp into Donald's car. She then took his hand and they started to walk the water's edge to the west. Drizzle continued to fall and the mist came down as they rounded the edge of the loch.

"Heck, Donald, I can only see about a hundred meters. If she's way out, we won't see a thing."

"Hayley reckoned Tink wouldn't move out too far due to her injury. Still, she did admit a lot of it was guesswork, so she could be wrong."

The going was slow as their scan was constantly broken when trying to negotiate the edge of the loch, uneven and rocky as it was. Kiera slipped on one occasion and only a fast hand from Donald saved her. Alas, her shoe was not soo fortunate as she dipped it fully under the water. Now as they walked, there was a squelching sound which broke the calm, peaceful silence along with the infrequent birdsong.

After a walk of an hour, they rounded a hillside entering a new loch. In total the expanse of water was about five football pitches and although the wind was calm, Donald saw motion on the water in excess of that which was expected. Kiera sat down and took off her wet shoe.

"Nothing here Donald. How far do you think she is expecting us to go?"

"Dunno, Kiera," answered Donald, eyes peeled on the water. There was a sense in him of a false stillness, like one made rather than natural. The birdsong had disappeared, at least from the immediate area. The butterflies stirred in his stomach.

"I'm exhausted Donald, maybe a wee wash will help me." Kiera stepped forward to the water and bent down hands cupped ahead of her and splashed water on her face. Keeping her eyes closed she let the fluid fall down her face and breathed in deeply. It felt good.

"Kiera don't move." Donald's voice was firm and deliberate. Kiera opened her eyes and stared into another face. Long, wet, black ringlets framed a fierce face which fixated on Kiera. Her eyes wandered past the gills on the neck to the powerful bare shoulders. A waxy chest of the same translucent skin as Tink's then gave way to the water. It was Kiera's first merman and he was very impressive.

His arm shot out and grabbed Kiera by the throat. Caught in his vice-like grip, Kiera immediately put two hands onto his wrists and tried to prise his arms apart. She heard Donald shout followed by the splash of his feet racing through the water towards them. Pain rather than a lack of air was her major problem and she felt her throat might be literally crushed to nothing. Throwing himself from five yards away, Donald performed a high rugby tackle on the merman knocking him backwards. The merman's grip remained tight on Kiera and she toppled into the water as well.

The loch hadn't appeared so but it was at least deeper than Donald was tall, for he found no footing and had to kick for the surface. As he broke the water, something thumped him hard across his hip and he lashed out but found nothing.

Now struggling for breath after the tumble, Kiera found her throat suddenly released and a pair of arms pushing her. She broke the surface and grabbed a rock beside her. Turning back to the water, she saw two heads, the merman and Donald, some twelve foot apart glowering at each other. Panic struck her as Donald was struggling just to keep himself above the water-line, clearly in no shape to take on the creature.

A head broke the water in the middle of the stand-off. Kiera recognised Tink's hair and then her face, as she turned toward the merman. Without fear or panic, she nuzzled her head under his chin before wrapping her arms around him. Noses touched and eyes met which seemed to calm the creature down. Who knew what was happening under the water but this was working.

"Donald, swim over here now, get out of the water."

Like I need an invite, thought Donald as he gave it his best front crawl to the shore. Kiera had hauled herself up by the time he joined her and she helped him until they fell together on the grass just clear of the loch. For a few moments they just breathed hard, lay on their backs watching the mer-couple carry out an intimate exchange.

"Donald, look at that. Just beautiful."

"Yeah and he clocked me a gorgeous one in the side too. That's going to bruise up. Are you okay?"

"Shush. Look at that. We're the first people to see that, mermaid love. Wish I had my camera."

"Kiera, your throat is well red. That's probably going to bruise."

"Would you shut-up about this stuff? Look at them. Just look. So like us, really, so like us."

Except for the tails, thought Donald, but decided his opinion was not ready to be received at the moment. He was engulfed in a surprising but deep kiss by Kiera which he was just about getting to grips with when she broke off. He saw the merman looking at him.

"Hold me, Donald, hold me."

"Sure, you frightened."

"Just hold me." Donald shifted his backside in an unattractive waddle until he was sat behind Kiera and wrapped his arms around her. She leaned back and kissed him. When he saw the merman again, Tink had placed herself with her back to her partner and the mer-man was wrapping his arms around her.

"So like us, do you see Donald?"

Donald saw but was having trouble reconciling this with the mermaid who had eaten so many fish over the last few days and made such awful sounds. So like us, he thought, yet so unlike us. I'm more confused than a British electorate.

There was definitely some form of smile on Tink's face, Kiera believed, and she was feeling warm inside despite being wet to the core. The last few days had held so much pain yet it was being coupled with so much wonder that it felt like a true explosion of life. Watching Tink begin to effect that howl which made no sense to a human, Kiera wondered what she was up to. The lens of her eye starting framing pictures of this joyous moment.

The surface of the water erupted and a multitude of heads broke the surface. Kiera couldn't count them all but there were at least fifty. All were mer-people, evident from the skin colour, and a few were males. The majority were however, females and all held something cradled in their arms. Flapping small tails led onto tiny torsos before emerging into slightly oversized heads. Some were bald, some with thin hair, others with the thickness of a gorse bush.

Jaw dropped, Donald gasped at the sight, trying to process what he was seeing. His first sense was one of wonder and excitement as he looked at each tiny face, feeling a man's protective drive coming to the fore. Then his brain countered with the thought of discovery of this nursery beneath the water. If people find this, there'll be television, scientists, all sorts of exploitation. And then if others find them first, they'll be nothing but a dead generation of mer-people. One mermaid in a bath tub was a near impossible to keep secret, this is something else.

"This is a privilege, Donald, such a privilege."

"It is Kiera, God knows it is." And God told us to take care of the animals.

# 20

# A New Place to Swim

"It would have been a better idea to put her back into the suitcase."

"No way, Donald. She is a creature and she needs looked after."

"Hayley, look you'll get no argument from me but there's a lot of places between here and where we are going. Lots of opportunities for her to be seen."

"We need to get her back into the water, sharpish too. Anyway, where are we going?"

"I don't know. Just away from here and any other civilised place."

A spattering of rain had obscured the windscreen and so while turning the ignition, Donald also hit the wipers. The blades smeared a greasy mess across.

"You really should clean the outside of your car, Donald. In fact clean the inside too."

"Hey, you put the fish woman in the back seat. I think you need to help out with the cleaning too."

Pulling away, Donald wondered how Kiera and Tommy would be getting on. It was no easy feat to get everything cleaned up, especially with the oncoming rush for the public meeting. Tommy had tried to ease Hayley's fears but his bravado was fairly transparent. Things were getting serious, thought Donald, and now was the time to act. Glancing round he saw that Tink had thrown the blanket over her backwards, exposing her torso.

"Hayley, can you sort her out. Bad enough seeing her head but any man's going to stop us if she sits up like that."

Giggling, Hayley covered Tink up to her neck with the blanket. Let's hope it stays light, thought Donald, things are just too serious.

Once clear of the car park, Donald headed through some back streets until he was able to take the main road out of the town heading west. Hayley was quiet and only the sound of his gear changes round severe corners and the occasional whimper from Tink broke the silence. The sky showed a darkening grey cloud and soon the spitting rain became steady. Island weather, does it ever change?

Rounding a corner, Donald had to apply his brakes as he saw a roadblock ahead. A young policewoman was indicating stop with a pronounced flat palm and eyeing the car intently. Blast, thought Donald, I can't get out of this. He rolled down the window as she advanced

"Excuse me sir, but we have reason to believe that someone is taking some items along this road that can help with our inquiries into an incident earlier today. Can I ask you to step outside and open your boot for me?" Her blonde hair was tied up and a pony tail came out from the back of her cap. She was of moderate height but had a slim figure. And her face, thought Donald, I know that face.

"Are you Joanne's sister?" asked Donald stepping from the

car.

"Joanne. Why yes. How did you know Joanne?"

"From school. The secondary in town. I used to sit beside her in Chemistry. You have her cheeks and eyes." The rain continued and Donald could hear a nearby river above the splatter of rain in the small puddle by the roadside. Bowing his head, he stared at his feet in remembrance of the vibrant blonde headed girl who he had chased but failed to win the heart of. She had been sixteen when she had collapsed at the school. Right beside him, just fell off her stool. He remembered the ambulance and so many people crying. What a waste of such a girl. To this day he still felt a rage at his helplessness, Mrs Macleod performing chest compressions while he stood in shock. Life was so cruel. It was only fair to fight against it.

"Donald, is it?"

"Yes, I was there that day. So sad. But you have her radiance, her beauty if you don't mind me saying so."

"No I don't. Thank you. I still need you to open the boot though."

"Oh, sorry, but of course." Stepping past the constable, Donald reached to open the boot but halted when the policewoman stopped and peered into the back seat window.

"Hey, is she okay? She looks somewhat pale."

"Oh her, she's fine. Just had a rough one last night, catching up on some sleep." The policewoman stared before coming round to the boot. Once opened, she scanned around the near emptiness.

"Okay Donald, that's fine. Have a safe trip and get your friend to her bed with some water."

"Will do. Thanks, Officer."

Donald quickly got into the car and continued the journey. Hayley kept glancing over. They started going through tighter corners and Tink sat up. The towel promptly fell off and Tink looked out the window.

Up ahead, Mr Morrison was returning his grandfather back to the home when the car had picked up a flat tyre. His father had insisted on standing out of the passenger seat on his own and was now just ahead and monitoring the traffic. The old man watched cars go past in the rain. Donald's car approached and the old man saw a car approach with an attractive young woman in the passenger seat. A blonde, her soft looking skin pulled at him. Continuing, he now saw the rear passenger seat. He thought he was going to collapse when he saw another blonde woman who appeared to be nearly nude. He chortled to himself.

"What's up Dad?" came his son's question.

"Young one's son, young ones. No end to what nonsense they get up to. Damn well like it."

"Whatever Dad. Hand me the wheel bolts."

A half hour after leaving the town, Donald was still none the wiser as to where to put Tink for safety. Hayley was suggesting one of the many little sea lochs around the island but they needed to find one without anyone nearby. By now they were far from any townships and it was the little isolated pockets of houses that were troubling their plans.

"Over there Donald. That's a sea loch."

"Blimey Hayley, there's just about no access down to the shore there. It's almost sheer cliffs. I don't think anyone even goes down there fishing."

"Perfect then. That's what we need. Find somewhere to

park her up and we'll make our way down."

There was a rough path down the hillside to the loch's edge. Not a path for humans but a sheep path. Donald had Tink over his shoulder and was wishing she had wings, for the long hours and lack of sleep were taking their toll on him. Struggling behind with her large veterinary bag, Hayley cursed the fact she only had her dress boots on. Although they could drive Tommy wild, they didn't have the necessary support for hillsides.

At the bottom of the slope was a very small beach of pebbles and a small cave, only a few paces deep but dry and well sheltered. Despite the rain, the area had a serenity as the waves lapped gently on the shore. Nodding her approval, Hayley placed her bag down and indicated for Donald to place Tink into the water. Hayley removed herself to inside the cave and was soon followed by Donald. Taking a seat beside her, Donald let out an enormous sigh.

"Shouldn't you get back and get some supplies for tonight. I dare say it won't be too warm out here."

"I will, I will, just give me a moment. Flippin' knackered Hayley. Anyway sorry to have to split Tommy and you. Think you have him well and truly caught." Hayley blushed. "I don't blame him. And thank you. We really needed your help. It's a heck of a risk you are taking. There's been too many people hurt already."

"And too many animals. Thanks Donald, you've been a real friend to Tink. What made you look after her in the first place? I mean why go to all that trouble?"

"Why are you here? Same reason. Right thing to do. And now I'm so deep in, I have to see it through. But it's easier when friends are with you."

"You realise it could be a week before Tink swims off. I don't think she'll leave the shallows until she is fit."

"Then we'd better get some sort of accommodation. Did you see any shielings round here?"

"You mean the little houses. The old summer ones for the peat cuttings. No I didn't."

"Okay, will need to think on that. I have some sleeping bags and blankets and that for tonight. I don't know if Tommy will get here. I'll go and get what's needed for here first before I think about getting the other two."

"If something does happen, at least she can flee now. She has a chance."

"Good. I hope so. There's too much violence going on at the moment. It's like a mermaid madness. Where's it going to end? Anyway, we can't change that at the moment, only keep Tink safe." Donald kissed Hayley's cheek in a friendly manner. It was obvious she didn't want to be on her own but there was no choice at the moment.

"Stay safe. And stay hidden if anyone comes. I'll be back soon." Hayley nodded.

She sat in the small cave watching the rain increase and pour down onto the loch in front of her, creating little circles of life, like a thousand fish grabbing food from the surface. Out of sight, she wondered if Tink was swimming about at all or just resting peacefully under the surface. As she began to feel cold, Hayley wrapped her arms closer to her chest and huddled her knees up to her chin. I hope Donald isn't long, she thought. Watching the loch closely from her distant position, she occasionally saw the flick of a tail. After an hour, Tink popped her head up and spotted Hayley in the cave. Hayley waved at her and Tink dived back under. This action was repeated and Hayley realised Tink was just making sure her friend hadn't left her.

There was an urge in Hayley to leap into the water and make sure Tink was okay. She wanted to look up close and examine the way she was moving her midriff, her tail, if she used her arms in the swimming action. How do they give birth, wondered Hayley? Mammal or fish? Eggs or live, and if live, where and when? And how do they do it when all is said and done? So much to learn about them, so much to interact with. And already we're at war. Such madness when there's so much wonder to be seen.

Hayley couldn't suppress her curiosity and began to strip off. Stuff it, there's no one out here and Donald should be a while. Leaving all her clothing in the cave, Hayley strode into the freezing loch water and began to swim out. Looking around for any significant ripple, any sign of Tink, she was in full abandonment to her work.

There was a blink of silver beneath her and she was able to fix onto Tink's curling beneath her. Hayley's eyes lit up and there was several minutes of sheer wonder before she was able to focus herself on a proper appreciation of the mermaid's movement. The constant background hum of the steady rain was broken with occasional splashes as Tink's tail broke the surface. Hayley was in a state of grace but was also concerned. Although this was her first mermaid, there was something forced about the swimming motion.

Tink came up close to Hayley and the vet caught her in her arms. The mermaid didn't struggle as Hayley examined her skin from tail to head. As a creature she was beautiful, graceful, lithe, yet with a fullness of figure. As Hayley ran her hands across Tink's shoulders, the creature reciprocated and

Hayley found herself staring deep into Tink's eyes looking for comprehension. *Just like a gorilla, I wonder how much of you is aware of this closeness, or do you just copy me?*

Hayley was so caught up in Tink, that the coldness of the water took her unaware. She stepped back to the shore feeling the water drop down to her waist and the chill air race across her chest. *Blimey, that's cold.* Then she heard the cough.

Hayley nearly shouted out but then caught Donald in the corner of her eye. He was turned away with a towel extended. Racing up to him, she grabbed the towel and ran into the shelter of the cave.

"Sorry Donald, I thought you would be a while yet."

"Hayley, I was two hours."

"Seriously. Oh, sorry. That was good of you not to look. Thank you."

"You really should be more careful. You can't just run around in the water with boobs exposed."

"Sorry Donald, alright. I know you have a thing with Kiera and I put you in an awkward situation but hey you didn't see anything, you acted like a gentleman, what's the big deal?"

"You can't do things like that!"

"Hey, don't freak out at me. I'm just a naked woman. Even if you caught a flash, what's the harm?"

"Hayley, don't you get it? It's not about me and if I saw anything. I'm a bloke, I can deal with nude women, I have the programming. It's the mermaids. You looked like one. Alyssa looked like one. You could get yourself killed."

The thought stopped Hayley in her tracks. In all her naivety, she never thought of the risk, the darkness surrounding the mermaids. How could they? How could she have been so dumb? A coldness overtook her. Clutching her towel, she curled herself into Donald's chest. At first he was a little bemused but on hearing her tears, he held her tight.

"I know Hayley, it's all wrong. I know. Dammit, I know."

# 21

# The Town Meeting

"Are there any more chairs anywhere, Tommy?"

The sports hall had its full quota of racked seating being utilised, pulled out from the recess in the wall like the side of a pyramid. Other seats had been placed facing the structure and a small lectern formed a focal point. The council leader, police chief and other noted office bearers were sat on these chairs, some shuffling quite nervously. Unusually for the police chief, he was in full uniform with radio clipped onto his lapel. Every minute or two he would talk briskly into the microphone, shaking his head.

The noise in the place was deafening as people passed the latest to each other, a gathering of nearly a thousand people, all with anxious thoughts. Shopkeepers, clergy, fishermen, school teachers and council employees had all gathered on the Sabbath. Only a few of the strictest observers had stayed away and such was the concern, no one even made mention of this breach of the traditional day of rest.

"No, the rest will have to stand, Kiera. I'm done, they need to get this thing started."

Kiera had stayed behind after tidying up, to give Tommy

a hand. A few people came up to her, telling how well she had done with that model girl, who had no right behaving like that on our beaches. Others commented on how shocked they were. The mood was certainly black if mermaids were mentioned. Kiera, however, was bemused at the populace's failure to notice the tinge of fish in the air. It was seemingly being dismissed due to the greater items to be attended to. Fortunate, thought Kiera, but then reminded herself that the greater items were what brought the people here.

"Have you heard anything? Hayley's not texted me," said Tommy.

"If they are keeping low, it's probably somewhere without a signal."

"Hope she's alright. She took the pictures on the telly real bad. She seems pretty sensitive, Kiera."

"Price of a kind heart, Tommy. She invests, Tommy, in what she believes." She saw Tommy's head drop. "Tommy, it's hard but you know what? She's invested in you. I ain't seen her like that with a guy before." Tommy nodded, smiled briefly and then went to the front of the hall to speak to the Council leader.

After sound checking, in a brutal fashion, of the microphones placed in front of the assembled leaders, the council leader stepped forward to speak. He waited patiently while the hubbub slowly faded and there was a silence, permeated only by the occasional cough.

"Good evening everyone, and thank you for coming out on this strangest of days. As you probably know, my name is Alan McAllister, and I am the current leader of the island council. With me, I have our chief constable, the head of the fisherman's union and other council heads of department. My thanks to the staff here at the leisure center for making this facility available at such short notice. Also I would like to …"

"Get on with it!" The shout was loud and sounded like a teacher addressing a tardy child.

"Yes, yes, I think a little patience …."

"Now, dammit. Say something of use for once in your life or sit down. In fact, just sit down McAllister and let the real people speak." This produced some murmuring and a few cackles of laughter but didn't deter the leader.

"Now is a time for calm and thought. These new creatures to our land and waters are largely unknown to us and we need time to assess and adapt to them."

"Assess!" a voice boomed out, "McCreddie's dead, assess that." Murmurs of agreement ran through the assembly.

"Yes he is, my friend. He is. And clearly these mermaids or mer-men, well, mer-people are dangerous. But so is a whale or a shark, so we must assess them." A faint ripple of applause died a quick death. "I'm going to hand over to our Chief Constable to explain the current situation and what people should do at this time. Chief Constable."

Chief Constable Jim MacIntyre was a thick set man in his late fifties, who was bemused at how his Sunday had suddenly exploded into a mythological riot, and which had stretched his small force to its limits. Actually, it was beyond their limits but best not to let that one out. After the initial riot in town, minor incidents of public law-breaking had continued and various shop windows were now broken. Clashes had occurred between animal rights protesters and angry local fishermen. None of this was going to be mentioned by the Chief Constable. This was a public calming exercise, showing a firm but reasonable controlling hand.

"Earlier today," announced CC MacIntyre flicking his moustache as he spoke, "a boat was sailed into the harbour with two incapacitated men and a younger man who was in a frightened disposition. Also on board was the body of a creature as yet not identified by our forensic team."

"Tell them it's a bloody mermaid!" came the cry.

"Mer-man, actually," came the reply from that pedantic clever clogs all crowds contain within them.

"Excuse me," continued CC MacIntyre, "but until the existence or not of those mythical creatures is established by scientists I shall refer to these animals merely as creatures. To continue, the injured men were taken to the island hospital where one unfortunately succumbed to his injuries. The younger man is helping with our enquiries and has indicated that they were attacked by a creature of the sea which is approximately the size of a man but with the tail of a fish."

"So it's a piggin' mermaid!"

"Mer-man!"

The policeman rolled his eyes, shook his head slowly and wiped his moustache with a thumb and forefinger. "At this time, we are advising all fishermen to assess if their trips are necessary and to take extra precaution when fishing. We believe the men may have interfered with the creatures in a deliberate fashion causing this incident but, nonetheless, all those who sail on the sea should be aware of the risk these creatures pose."

"We need a cull! Damn bloody things. How we meant to fish? It's our livelihood."

"No one is to take undue action. I stress again," MacIntyre's eyes scanned the crowd, "no one is to take undue action, that is, to go on the offensive. Defend yourselves by all means but do not seek out these creatures." He paused, assessing if his words had taken effect. "There was also an incident at the harbour this afternoon were a crowd took it upon themselves to riot and procure the body of the dead creature from our incident tent. I know some of you are here and I say this to you. You are holding back the investigation of this matter by the relevant authorities. I request the body be returned and my force be allowed to deal with this situation in the manner it should be dealt with. This is a general call but if necessary the full resources of the law will be used to pursue those who are taking matters into their own hands."

"Have you got any Necromancers?" asked a black haired teenager.

"I'm sorry."

"Have you got a Necromancer?"

"Necromancer? What are you on about, son?"

"Well they took it up Pike's hill and after kicking the shit out of it, they burnt it to dust. Bloody stank too." The crowd erupted in a mixture of disgust and howls of delight. Vengeance and despair at humanity sat side by side in blue plastic chairs.

"Settle! Calm down! And mind the language," shouted the Chief Constable, his voice elevated to an almost indistinguishable white noise with the closeness of the microphone. But the gathering continued with its debate and soon voices were becoming wilder and threats were being passed. Despite there being no animal rights activists in the room, a measure dictated by MacIntyre, the respective rights of animal and man were causing a community to implode in its own leisure center.

Local arguments became extremely heated as it became

apparent that the farmed fishing nets had been broken into, allegedly by mer-people. The main core of the debates expanded to include territorial disputes, the effect of incomers to the island and how the police were an oppressive force anyway.

The first metaphorical punch was thrown by a fisherman of about sixty years old who clocked a teenager across the cheek with an open handed slap. He never saw the fist of the young man's father as it knocked two front teeth out. A policeman stepped in drawing his nightstick, much to MacIntyre's horror, before hitting the father across the back of the legs. That was the trigger for a free-for-all and soon blue plastic chair bases left their fixed positions to fly across the sports hall as high as the shuttle cocks that get smacked back across the courts on an average Saturday.

Police constables waded into the situation as Tommy and the few other center staff tried to shield and escort older attendees out of fire exits and any other available passages. An elderly lady was knocked to the ground in front of Kiera and she reached down for the woman, pulling her back up before supporting her out of the nearest door. This took them into the café area and Kiera guided the woman to a chair before surveying her for any damage. Blood was pouring out from a large split in the front of the woman's left tight.

"Hang on, dear. I'll be right back." Kiera raced to the office and grabbed a green first aid box from the wall. On her return, she had to circumvent two middle aged men trying to plant flailing hooks on each other. The woman was still in the chair but was bent double and her broken, choked sobbing was audible even over the chaos next door.

"Oh love, it's you. I thought you'd gone. Oh dear, thank

you."

"Leg up Missus, we need to get this patched up. Are you feeling any other pain?" A trembling no was the answer. With a practised ease, Kiera swiftly cleaned and bandaged the wound. As she looked up into the lady's face she could see a queue of people sat beside them.

"Kiera," shouted Tommy, pointing at the seated injured, "can you?" Kiera nodded. She worked hard amidst the fighting going on around her and several men formed a ring, preventing anyone coming into the circle who was looking for trouble. Over time the situation simmered down, people drifted away or were taken by van to be kept at Her Majesty's pleasure. Ambulances came and went, concerned relatives arrived until at last the center was cleaned up to a fashion and Tommy thanked his staff before making sure they had a safe ride home.

"Some day, Kiera." Tommy had switched all the lights off except for one lonely lamp in the café. Standing in front of the table where Kiera was sat, he offered her a cup of tea from the machine.

"Thanks Tommy. Is that it then? All done, all cleaned up?"

"Yes, and thanks Kiera. You did really well with all those injuries. Regular trooper, you." Kiera smiled. Then she started to weep. Gently, holding back the flood but still little rivers of water fell from her cheeks onto her jeans.

"You okay?" asked Tommy. "What's wrong? It's all done now, Kiera, all over."

"As if Tommy, as if." The vehemence in her voice surprised her and she saw him turn his head away. "Tommy," she whispered in a softer tone, "sorry, that wasn't meant for you. That was for.... well, for all this crap. How when something so beautiful arrives do we end up like this? How?"

Tommy shrugged. He had seen neighbours pitched against neighbours, locals against incomers, police versus the ordinary citizen and youth taking on the old, all this without any animal rights activists in the building. Closed tomorrow, thought Tommy. He reckoned this was a wise move and he could pop in and assess the damage to the building. Equipment had been tampered with and he couldn't be sure what was fit for purpose without a thorough inspection. The boss would be delighted.

"Did you hear what they said, Kiera? Some of those friends of McCreedie. Going hunting for mermaids. Tink's not safe."

"Tink? Never mind Tink, Donald and Hayley aren't either. You saw what this thing has done to people, it's like popcorn at the moment. One going off here, then one there, then all the bits going at once. Soon the lids going to blow off this. Alyssa might be just the first of many incidents."

"Has he texted or phoned?"

"Not yet."

"What do you want to do?"

"Honestly Tommy? I want to say piss off to the whole place and grab Donald, take him to somewhere happy and gorgeous and just try to love each other without all this nonsense."

"Would be nice, Kiera, would be nice." His eyes drifted upward, an image of Hayley forming on a deserted beach. Yeah, Tommy thought, would be nice.

"I had a friend here, Christine, she would have been horrified at all this. But she wouldn't have been surprised. People are like sheep, she told me once. They need something to follow, to show them where to go. But a few are rams and lord it over the others. Some are sheepdogs, rounding people up and pointing them in a direction. Very few are the farmer directing the sheepdog. They like their wool to have a colour on it, to belong. To be directed. To let someone else make the call, make the moral judgement. All the time showing a large fleece with the colour on it. But sometimes they get sheared, she said to me. Only then do you see the real sheep. Only then are we truly exposed. That's what the mermaids are doing Tommy. Shearing us. Exposing us. I don't like what I see."

"There's nothing here to do, Kiera, least not until tomorrow. Do you want to go find them? I know it's near midnight and they could be anywhere but..... It's better than just not trying. They might not need us but I don't know that."

"I couldn't care if he needs me or not, I need him. Come on stud, let's go."

"Does she call me stud? Wow!"

"Actually she doesn't, just thought you needed the lift." Tommy threw Kiera's jacket over her head.

# 22

# Hunting Party

An acrid whiff of peat smoke filled the nostrils of each man as they took up a seat in the front room of Angus McCreedie, brother of the deceased fisherman. Due to the number, in excess of twenty, the seats in question were a variety of stools, work benches and a three piece dilapidated sofa, stilling sporting a faded seventies floral pattern. All were silent and the ornamental clock above the mantel piece told every beat of its mechanical heart. Closest to the fire sat Angus, his son opposite, and at his shoulder the recently bailed Iain McClaren.

"Gentlemen, thank you for coming at this late hour and for your condolences for my brother. Many of us are fishermen and those of you who are not are well aware of the dangers of the sea. We take our lives in our hands daily on the waves. But now, we have a different threat. These fish men and women, these brutal abominations, clearly not God-designed, seek us out. Rest assured they see us as a threat to their kingdom, their fish. Well it's not theirs'."

Angus McCreedie stared into the fire as a general hum of accord passed around the room. The man behind him placed a firm hand on Angus' shoulder. His son stood up and reaching into a dresser on the side removed a large number of shot glasses. Quickly they were passed around the assembly, with a bottle of malt following to charge the glasses.

"To John, God rest his soul."

"To John," came the unanimous reply.

A second bottle was passed around. Angus took to his feet and with one arm leaning on the mantel, his legs warming from the fire, he faced the gathered men. His eyes were heavy and his manner grim. No one spoke or coughed, all holding respect to this giant of the fishing world. In a faded black shirt, opened at the neck and in blue jeans too wide at the bottom, he surveyed each one of the men. All good lads, he thought.

"I once heard the story of a man who had a dog with lice. He didn't believe in those fancy shampoos or cleaners and so he decided he would carefully take off every lice on the dog and make it clean again. Days he would spend hunting them and he removed so many that the dog looked better. For a season, it was well and healthy. But then the lice came back. So the man started again.

Again he picked off every lice he could find on the dog but once again they came back the following season. For five years he repeated this. Then in his sixth year he realised one day that the dog's blanket seemed alive. The blighters were all over it. So the man burnt the blanket. This time when he had cleaned the dog, it remained clean.

Understand me, gentlemen, there are these creatures about and we need to eradicate them. We need to search our lochs and coves for them before hunting in the sea. But know this, until we find where they are coming from, we will not defeat them, only prolong it. But tonight we hunt. We hunt mermaid.

Are you with me, lads?" And the glasses dropped their liquor to show a resounding yes.

Hayley was cold. Her feet had lost all feeling after the small fire built by Donald had died. It was too dark now to see anything outside, and anyway, she was determined to remain beneath the blankets. Wrapped up in a fleece she should have felt warmer but her dip in the sea with Tink had left her chilled and she hadn't recovered. Donald's back was up against hers and she felt the shared warmth under the blanket but this was as close as Kiera's man would allow himself to be. No wonder, she thought, it will start to look like I am hitting on him. He hadn't even complained when she had inadvertently farted.

The wind was blowing across the entrance to their small cave and the shrill sound was keeping her awake. She had listened out for Tink but had now reckoned the mermaid was asleep, probably underwater as she seemed to be capable of breathing in two fashions. How this was achieved puzzled her but without a dissection she wasn't sure any hypothesis could be confirmed. And there had been enough bodies already.

There it was. The faint motor of a car. And then switched off. Someone was out there. Hayley sat up to see if she could hear better but the wind continued its whistling. There was a voice. It was faint but male. She tapped Donald gently but got no response. Reaching up, she started to tweak his ear lobe. A smack from a hand was his only reply. She bent close down to his ear and said as loud as she could, "Donald." He started to shake himself awake.

As Donald turned to her in puzzlement, she pointed outside the cave to a beam of light sweeping ahead of them. Sitting up, Donald reached for his jacket, slipping it quietly on. Two figures passed across the cave front, one thick set with a smaller, thinner legged individual walking behind.

"Don't you recognise that backside, Hayley? I know the other one," whispered Donald. Hayley looked at him bemused. "Tommy," shouted Donald, "she forced me in her, trying to have her wicked way."

The torch flashed round and lit up the cave. Kiera ran inside and leapt on Donald, cuddling him tightly before kissing. Tommy reached for Hayley and they embraced.

"How was the meeting?" asked Donald.

"Bad," answered Tommy, "well bad. Lot of fighting, the center is pretty messed up." Kiera didn't add to this but instead climbed under the blankets and snuggled up to Donald. "Best left to tomorrow. I'm exhausted, it's three a.m."

"Good idea, Tommy, I need warmed up," Hayley said, pulling Tommy even closer.

"Easy Tiger," laughed Tommy, "I just found you in bed with another man. Explanations before fun and games, Madam!" He copped a slap to the side of his head, before some hungry arms sought him further. Sleep soon engulfed them all.

"Do we have enough for everyone?"

"Yes, Dad. Between shotguns, a few hunting rifles and some knives, everyone's been armed."

"Good. Son, go and bring them all together. Then we'll get this under way." Angus MacCreddie's son turned away, obeying his father's instruction while the fisherman lit a cigarette. John had been an ass of a brother, all told. Always getting himself into messes he shouldn't have and now he'd paid for it. But this was blood and blood had to be avenged. Dragging around carcasses through town wasn't the thing.

No, this was going to turn into a cull. Pushing those beasts back from our lochs. Protecting our fish and waters from these invaders. Our daughters from their topless parading of their charms, flaunting it, encouraging the young ones to be as vulgar. No, this sort of thing wasn't done here. So now was the time to change it. To protect. But above all to pay them back for John.

"Everyone's ready Dad."

"Okay, men. You know what to do. You have your routes to follow. Keep your eyes peeled and if you see something, telephone in. If there's no signal then use the radio. But remember code words. Phone then radio. We can't let what we are doing get out. Not until it's done. Not until they see why we did it. Not until it's better. Good hunting!"

Slowly, a grey light was forcing back the darkness, revealing a misty morning which was damp and cold. Into this blandness of grey drove eleven vehicles, mostly off-road 4x4s, with the singular purpose to find and kill. Looking out of her window, the octogenarian housed next to Angus McCreedie wondered what all the fuss was about. Given the events she had heard on the news, she decided not to investigate but instead to put the kettle back on.

Angus rode in the passenger seat beside his son, eyes staring ahead, pondering how long the task would take. There was little traffic on the road, not surprising for an early Monday morning. There'll probably be little traffic all day after word of the meeting at the leisure center gets out. The radio chattered with minor reports of a few hunters arriving at their search points. No place names were used and nothing to give away anyone's identity. Most reports will probably be by radio, thought Angus. Annoying because the messages could be intercepted but an unfortunate necessity due to the remoteness of the island and its coast.

"Golden Eagle, Puffin has seen the fish, ready to engage." Angus "Golden Eagle" MacCreedie looked down at the map on his lap and shouted at his son to head towards Vatilisker point, approximately ten miles from town. Given their current location, Angus estimated a five minute drive. Fortune favours us then, first call and we're right beside it.

Turning down a mere track, Angus' 4x4 soon came up on a Land-rover driven by "Puffin". The muck from its route showed across the wheel hubs of the vehicle and Angus scoured the vista for its owner. He could see him down near the water's edge behind a rock with his compatriot beside him. Lifting his binoculars, he also saw the green sheen of skin and then tail breaking the surface of the water. The red hair of the creature was long, touching where a human bottom would be, and on turning round it was obviously a mermaid.

So it was one of these creatures that did for John. Angus could understand the attraction of catching one, why John had tried but he knew he wouldn't be doing the same. Slowly, he climbed out of the passenger door and grabbed his rifle from the boot. He carefully loaded his ammunition before walking quietly towards his hunters. As the wind was blowing away from the sighting, he had no fear of his smell giving his presence away. Reaching the rock, he sat down beside the hunter. The grass was wet and the ground covered in dew but he didn't care.

"Just the one, Angus" reported the hunter. Taking position and resting his rifle on the rock and his shoulder, Angus tried to sight the creature. Leaning the rifle into him he muttered the words, " One from John, you bitch." The trigger was pulled but just as it reached its full displacement, the creature moved, diving into the water as the report echoed round the loch-side. "Dammit." Angus realised this wasn't going to be a quick hunt but more of a prolonged cull. He grabbed the binoculars again and saw her swimming out towards the open sea. Maybe we'll need to go to boats at some point.

He knew boats would be a risk, given the mermaids obvious advantage. John and his crew were taken out and possibly by just the one merman. Staying on land was the safer option and besides, they didn't have boats they could risk. You didn't pick up a fishing boat that easy. The trawlers would be too big when they needed fast out-boarders.

Telling "Puffin" well done and to continue with the search, Angus retreated back to the car. Only an hour's hunting and a sighting already. Things were going to plan. If the boys in the town could keep the police busy, then this might just work.

# 23

# Narrowing of the Sights

Hayley was scanning in earnest across what little water she could see in the increasing fog. The blanket of wispy fluff that previously surrounded the hills, had descended so that the horizontal line of sight was now a few hundred meters. Looking upward, the hillsides were still visible, set in the dank, grey clouds of drizzle.

Hacked off behind her, Tommy reflected that if he didn't know the woman in front and hadn't been deeply interested in furthering a relationship with her, he would have waved goodbye some time ago. As it was, he was feeling damp, a little cold and fed up. Didn't she realise he had a job to go back to, assessments of damage to make. How did he end up here when it all started with a night of supposed raunchy fun? Not that it hadn't been fun at times. But at times it had been brutal. As he watched her perfect cheeks wiggle in stride, he acknowledged he was going nowhere. You're smit, Tommy my son, smit.

"Where is she? Tommy, anything, can you see anything?"

"Keep looking, babe. She'll turn up. Just keep looking."

Tommy's mind wandered off Hayley's backside and he

looked ahead, fearing any impasse to their progress. Often at these rock-sides there would be places of small sheer cliffs which would require a detour, not long in distance but with a decent climb. They'd been past two already and he was waiting for the next one to further spoil his day.

Then out of the mist came a pair of figures. Seeing only the tip of a shotgun extending past a person's shoulder, Tommy instinctively grabbed Hayley and drew her close. His hand shot over her mouth before she could complain and as the figures gained more definition, he sat on a rock, pulling Hayley down onto his lap. He tilted her head so as to kiss her but keep his eyes on the advancing men. A brief exchange of pointing between the men told Tommy they had been spotted and he swept his hands under Hayley's top.

Breaking the kiss, Tommy whispered in Hayley's ear, "There's two guys coming with a shotgun. When I start to talk to them, adjust yourself to make this look real."

"Feels pretty real to me."

Tommy ignored the jibe and focused on the men. The bright orange waterproofs that they were wearing reminded Tommy of those he had seen on the fishing boats. The man on the left was significantly older with a bushy beard, while the other was a younger man, maybe even a teenager given his spotty complexion.

"No need to perve," hissed Tommy as they approached.

"Romantic place to take a woman," goaded the bearded man, "the dump not open today." His laugh made up for the lack of anyone else finding it funny.

"It was until you interrupted," frowned Hayley, reaching under her top and adjusting as requested. "No need to bring guns out to go snooping on couples anyway."

"We're hunting mermaids, not snooping," said the young man, fixated at Hayley's movements. A dig in the ribs from his partner soon drew him back.

"Where you going to find them round here? The news said it was a fishing boat that found that one," asked Tommy.

"Don't you worry about that, son," said the older man. "Take it you ain't seen one then."

"Got my hands full with Kate here. Don't need another woman however they show themselves. If you don't mind." The older man turned away but the younger one lingered before following. "I wouldn't mind, Davie, would you?" was heard over the shoulders and Tommy embraced Hayley again.

"What do we do about them?" whispered Hayley in Tommy's ear.

"Just keep up the pretense for a few more minutes in case they are watching."

"Bet that younger guy's watching."

"Hayley, just keep up the façade. We need them to move on."

"Did you see how he ... " But Tommy had got back into full acting mode. It was five minutes later when he broke off and looked around him. Satisfied they were alone again, he tapped Hayley's backside indicating she should rise but she stayed put.

"Tommy, they had shotgun."

"I saw. This is getting dangerous, very dangerous."

"They're heading to where Tink was earlier, Tommy if they see her." Hayley was starting to shake a little now and was staring at Tommy hoping for some solution.

"I don't know where she is? We are as blind about this as they are. Hayley, what do you want to do? I mean is she likely to be back there. Or should we just continue on ahead."

"We could track them. Stop them before they do anything."

"Hayley, they have a bloody shotgun. I mean you don't go out hunting mermaids everyday with a shotgun. A net's normal but a shotgun." Tommy's mind pointed out to him that his use of the word normal with mermaid hunting was a worrying development and any further links like this could require him seeing someone professional.

"Tommy, they'll kill her. Just kill her."

"So you think we should trail them," queried Tommy.

"Well, I'm going to."

"No way, you're as subtle as a toddler in a paddling pool. No way. I ain't having you get shot on me."

"Stop me then." Hayley went to walk off but Tommy grabbed her to him.

"I'll go. Come with me until we get near to the car and then you get in, get somewhere with a signal and get the police, okay. They won't want some vigilantes walking around with shotguns."

Hayley looked into his eyes and then kissed him gently on the lips. "Thank you. She's worth it. She's a beautiful creature."

"She's not the beautiful creature I'm doing it for." He took her hand and led her back along the shore.

"Look at them, Donald. Barely a few days old."

"How do you know that? They could be any age."

"Well they look like a few day's old human baby. Except for the tails of course." Kiera had been fawning for the last two hours and kicking herself for not having a camera with her. Donald had long since begun to dry and sort out their clothes but they were still wet through. They were both in their underwear as Donald tried to slap the clothes on rocks and wring them to a drier state. Theoretically helping, Kiera was too engrossed in their discovery.

Tink was swimming in amongst the other mermaids but her attention kept refocusing on the merman who had attacked them earlier. Kiera and Donald whilst on friendlier terms with the creature, were maintaining a distance from the edge of the loch. The animal instinct for survival in all humans conquering any reconciliation attempt they felt they should make.

"Heck Davie, all the freak shows are out today."

Kiera turned and saw the young man looking at her in his orange waterproofs. Instinctively she covered her underwear with her hands, fending off his eyes with an angry stare.

"Hell Davie, mermaids!"

The young man ran up to the water and was being followed by an older man with a bushy beard. The man took a bemused look at Kiera and Donald in their underwear, before spying the mermaid nursery.

"Damn, McCreedie's going to love this."

Kiera was surprised to see the man then fall forward, hitting the ground face first. Tommy was stood behind holding a large rock but dropped it immediately to grab the shotgun, now on the ground. The young lad turning watched Tommy aim it right between the young man's eyes.

"You ever touch my girl and I'll blow your balls off, mate."

"Tommy, thanks. Where's Hayley?"

"Gone to get the police. We came across these two hunters and thought we had better track them. Sounds like there's a lot more of them too. What have you two been up to? Where's your clothes?"

"We found Tink, Tommy," answered Kiera, "tracked her here. Unfortunately her boyfriend got a tad angry at first and we ended up scrapping in the pool. But it's sorted now, though I wouldn't go too near the edge."

"You guys must be cold. Hey, you who was perving my girlfriend, take the waterproofs off and throw them to her. Nothing funny or I'll shoot." Tommy had a face like thunder and Donald was worried he might actually carry out the threat. Stood in his boxers, he didn't feel like he could give a steadying word without looking totally ridiculous. Turning the man with the beard over, Donald stripped him of his waterproofs and dragged him to one side.

"The big man's rucksack, Donald, check it for rope," instructed Tommy.

"Yeah, there's some here." Tying up the young man first, followed by the larger man, Donald then tied their shoelaces together. Kiera was sat on a rock with a worried look on her face.

"You think there's more, Tommy?" asked Kiera.

"Well, he mentioned a McCreedie. The dead man was McCreedie. Could be there's a posse out, after all you saw how hot the temperature was at the leisure center."

"That makes it complicated. Looking after one mermaid was hard enough but we got whole families here. Or shoal or whatever we call them."

"Do you think we could shoo them away?" asked Donald. "Seems to me the safest place to be is the sea, far out and deep."

"I don't think they want to go," Kiera said, standing and wrapping her arms around Donald, "after all they chose here to have babies."

"They spawn here," asked Tommy wide eyed, "how come no one's ever seen them before?"

"Maybe this is their first time," postured Donald, "maybe something's brought them here."

"Bit X-files with that thinking, mate."

"And mermaids are normal how, Tommy?"

"Hayley would have a better guess, Tommy," said Kiera, "Best wait until she gets here, she shouldn't be long if she was only popping to the car."

Watching the yellow plane land from the terminal, Laura felt herself fortunate that her husband hadn't been going away on the return journey. The yellow beech-craft with their twin engines served the islands as air ambulances, supplemented by helicopters as the need arose. Laura was welcoming a girl she had just gotten to know. Poor Alyssa with her dreams of modelling glory smashed apart by that troubled boy. Still, James had been good to her. I hope there's more to it than troubled times, thought Laura.

Making her way to the apron where the aircraft would park, Laura could see the ambulance waiting to take Alyssa back up to the local hospital. Once there, she would probably get discharged within an hour or two if all was well. The beech-craft taxied onto the apron, its engines disturbing the windless day before shutting down and Laura watched from the perimeter fence trying to get a glimpse of her guest. The door that flipped down to provide steps opened and a medic, followed by James, stepped off. Laura was surprised to see Alyssa exit the aircraft unassisted. James was quickly to her side providing support but as they approached the ambulance, they were ordered back to the aeroplane.

There was little protest as the blue lights of the ambulance started to flash and its siren wailed to the air. Within a minute, the vehicle had exited the airport heading for its new cause. Standing next to James, the medic seemed concerned and was pointing at the various buildings in the airport. Constantly waving for their attention, Laura finally made a connection with Alyssa. She nudged James and he began to walk over to Laura.

"Hi, how are you Mrs McKinney? Everything okay."

"Hi James, good to see you and also Alyssa on her feet. I take it you have seen the news."

"Yes. The riot seems like a bad do altogether. A few hurt they said."

"There was and my Murdo was one of them. Got kicked to pieces by the crowd covering up an animal rights activist. But he'll live."

"No way! That's dreadful. There's too many things kicking off. Anyway, we have a problem. The ambulance has just had a 999 call and apparently they are coming back here to put the patient straight on the plane. The other ambulances are busy so we are going to have to wait. It's a pain because basically once up there, Alyssa is going to get discharged to come back in for day clinics. I think we are going to sit in the terminal."

"Can I take you up? Would that be alright, save you sitting around?"

"Thanks, Mrs McKinney, I'll ask."

"Good, and it's Laura, James. No need for any of the Missus nonsense."

Disappearing back to the aircraft, it took several minutes' negotiation and a telephone call to the hospital to make the arrangements. Once the plans were agreed, the medics offered Alyssa a wheelchair which she politely declined before taking James' arm and walking out of the perimeter gates to greet Laura.

"Look at you girl, on your feet. Wow, you're doing well."

"It's nice to be clear of the hospital down in Glasgow. All we got was reporters, reporters and more reporters. Just because you pose topless, doesn't give some of those sleaze-balls the right to ask some of the questions they come out with. One guy actually made me an offer for an explicit magazine, I had to stop James for flooring him."

"But you're healing, dear. That's good. You can get plenty of rest now and relax. These things take time. I'm sure you're sore and who knows what else has scarred you."

"I do get nightmares, Laura. Dreams of being hunted. But he hasn't left my side. James has been a real help."

"Well I wish you all the best on that front. Now shall we get you up to be discharged?" Laura's car was small and James was cramped up in the back seat along with their luggage. He had pushed Alyssa's seat right back and denied himself room.

"You okay to stretch out? Got enough room, Als?"

Als is it, thought Laura, they really are getting on. As Laura steered the car out of the airport car park, Alyssa continued to tell of her harassment by the media. She also talked of how she had received flowers from all sorts of people as well as some hate letters from people who said she deserved it all for being a tart. Laura listened patiently trying not to fire out her own deeply held views. Here to help, Laura reminded herself, here to help. A buzzing sound distracted her and she wondered where it was coming from. It was low in tone and seemed to be some sort of vibration.

"Laura, have you got a mobile phone?" asked James.

"Yes, but I rarely use it, only to tell Murdo I'm late. But they are great things. Why do you ask?"

"Because that's a mobile phone sounding and it's not mine."

"And I haven't one on me. Stops me getting any dodgy calls," Alyssa added.

"It should be in my hand bag, Alyssa. Near the top. Can you get it? I know you shouldn't speak on it when you're driving." Leaning forward, Alyssa strained and let out a low moan as she felt her shoulder twinge before pulling the black handbag onto her lap. Taking out the mobile, she examined the screen.

"It's Kiera, Laura."

"Well, speak to her dear, I can't."

"No, it's a text."

"Oh, never use that. What's she say?"

"Blimey Laura, get police, little loch west of loch Erstforth. Hunters with guns after mermaid. Please help." Laura slammed on the brakes. Cars behind her desperately copied her and then sat in disbelief as the little car in front of them did a wild, three point turn before blazing off again. Horns hooted as soon as senses were regained.

"It's okay, Alyssa, the station's this way."

## 24

# Captured

Well that's one line of attack done anyway, thought Hayley, as she saw the time appear beside the message indicating that it had been sent. Good job Kiera's mobile was in the car. With Tommy on my network and no signal from it, I'd have been well stuffed. Not that there's much from Kiera's either, can't even maintain connection to ring through. Still, I'll take the car up a bit and see if the signal doesn't improve. I hope Mrs McKinney understands.

A crunch of a twig caused Hayley to turn around. A strong man in waterproofs holding a rifle smiled at her.

"Sorry to bother you love, but you're a bit far out." Hayley stumbled backwards before composing herself. Damn, I'd hoped to meet no one else.

"Just getting away from it all," said Hayley nervously. "Been a bit crazy in town lately."

"Yes, it has. Damn mermaids," hissed McCreedie. "You out her alone?" The man advanced towards Hayley threatening her personal space. Dripping wet and stinking of sweat, he cast his eyes up and down Hayley.

"No," answered Hayley, a little too forcefully. "There's a

few of us, I'm just off to get some bits and pieces."

McCreedie seemed appeased. "Have you seen any mermaids down by the loch? You need to be careful, some will take a man's life."

"Right, I'll keep that in mind." Hayley tried to step past the man to Tommy's car but he grabbed her arm.

"Hey, what you playing at?"

"I asked, had you seen any mermaids? You didn't answer. Have you seen any?" McCreedie pulled Hayley close to his face and stared into her eyes. Shaking her head, Hayley tried to draw away. The grip on her arm remained tight and Hayley drew her head down as McCreedie continued to stare.

"You knows something girl. You're way too quiet. Tell me what you know or I'll have to find out from you. And you won't like that." Just then a younger man approached from behind the trees.

"Can't raise the team from down here on the radio. So I reckon we.... who the hell's that?"

"Just some girl I found lingering. Reckon she knows something too."

"Hang on Dad, that's the vet. Oh yeah, recognise her alright now. Don't forget that figure in a hurry."

"Okay lady, what are you doing here? Tell me now." Hayley summoned all her nerve.

"If you must know, I'm out here with the council leader for a bit of fun. Sex. And he's going to be mighty pissed to find out you're threatening his woman. So I suggest you let me go before he finds out." The harsh grip released and Hayley made her way directly to the car door. Opening it, she jumped inside and fumbled the car keys out of her pocket. Turning the ignition on, she floored the accelerator but hadn't dropped the clutch sufficiently and the wheels spun on the grassy path.

"Hang on, Dad, I thought the news said the council leader was delivering a statement at the town hall just now."

"The wee bitch!"

The car lurched forward as McCreedie's son tried to step towards it and he was caught on the left knee, spinning him round before falling to the floor. His father ignored him and aimed his rifle as Hayley drove away up the track. A shot rang out and the back windscreen blew out with a piercing crash. Hayley panicked, thinking she had been shot, and her hands slid round the steering wheel causing the car to fight against its current momentum. The vehicle slid off the track and walloped into a tree.

Stepping over his son, McCreedie bounded towards the car, which was lodged against a stout trunk, driver's side against it. Inside he saw Hayley slumped towards the wheel with the deflated air-bag lying between. From the side of her head he saw some blood but was undeterred as he flung open the passenger door and reached across. Grabbing her blonde hair, he yanked the girl from the car, letting her fall to the wet ground.

"Right, where are they? Where are they?"

There had been a pain banging in her head before she felt her hair being yanked. Everything hurt and her ears were ringing from the explosion that had happened when she was still on the road. Opening her eyes, she saw the man shouting at her, but there was no sound. There was only the warping fog of a wall of noise. Then she saw a rifle being pointed in her face. And then blackness.

"Damn it, she's fainted. Do you hear me, son? She's fainted." There was a wailing from down the track. McCreedie saw his son rolling around, holding his knee, almost in tears. "Would you get up? Hell, you'll live. Get your sodding arse over here and give me a hand." The only response was a further wail. Gotta sort everything out myself damn it, thought McCreedie. Dragging Hayley to the side of the tree, he propped her up against it.

With one hand on her chin, he started slapping her cheeks, advising her to wake up. With no response coming, McCreedie increased the venom of his strike and marks started appearing on Hayley's cheek. Swooning around, consciousness returned slowly to Hayley, and her ears began to hear normally.

"Where are they? Where did you see them? Tell me girl or I'll drop you into the loch with some rocks. They killed my brother and they need sorting, so don't be daft, just tell me. Dammit, tell me!" The last comment came along with a backhanded swipe that drew blood from Hayley's mouth. Part of her wanted to resist but self-preservation made her point towards what she thought was the shore. "They're hardly going to be inland, you stupid cow, where?" Another backhand swipe.

"Sh.... shore...... at the shore."

James, although sitting in the back seat, was in a state of terror at Laura's driving. Blind overtaking, horn honking to get rid of any unfortunate traffic happily obeying the Highway Code but on the particular side Laura happened to be on at that moment. Conversely Alyssa, whilst holding her shoulder due to the occasional painful bump, was directing and pointing out obstacles. There was even a smile on her face.

"Not far now, Alyssa," announced Laura, "round the next two bends and there."

"If they don't pull you in before that!" announced James.

"When we get there, I'll drop you two off and you can explain. Wow, where did he come from? You two round up the troops and then follow me out there."

"No way, Mrs McKinney, you don't know what you're going to run into."

"I'm a minister's wife, James, I think I've seen my fair share of nasty."

"No, I'm going with you. Alyssa can talk to the police. It's not like they don't know her. Watch your wing mirror!"

"It's fine. Never use it anyway."

"I don't use them either. James should go with you, Laura. It'll be safer. I'll be fine."

"Are you sure, dear?"

"Yes, and I'll let them know about the side of that Audi as well. Just drop me."

"And here," announced Laura. "Praise the Lord."

"He's definitely on your side," said James looking back up the road at the scene of destruction.

"I'll be there soon," said Alyssa stepping out of the car. "Got the phone. Stay safe, James. Get going."

James had wanted to swap seats and take over the driving. Such was the speed of the drop-off, he was still in the back seat when Laura unleashed the little engine and began to terrorise the island's road users again.

Alyssa surveyed the front doors of the police station and quickly entered the reception. The journey from the airport, although short, had been a painful one and she was feeling a little weak as she approached the front desk. With a bing, she summoned help and was greeted by a young male constable.

"Good morning Madam, how can I help you?"

"Well, I need a posse of policemen, some 4x4s and probably some form of weaponry."

"Okay, any particular reason." Alyssa threw Laura's mobile in front of the constable.

"I have friends in trouble. There could be killings." The policeman looked closely.

"You're that girl who was harpooned. The topless model. Ah, I recognise you now. From the investigation reports, of course. Hold on, I'll just get my Sergeant."

Within a minute, Alyssa was telling her tale to the Sergeant and then the chief constable. It was evident to Alyssa as she spoke that there was debate raging in the Chief's head.

"Forgive me Chief, but what's the big problem here. Why ain't we on our way yet?"

"You see, Miss, we have a tinderbox here in the town at the moment. I daren't deploy any of my people so far out."

"But there's guns involved. It's Kiera we are talking about. She saved my life."

"I appreciate that but there's been no mermaids reported round that way. The press would have a field day if it all kicked off and we were miles away."

"And fail to save the hero of the paper model and what? Especially if there's guns. And a mermaid blood-bath. I think the press would eat you for that one." The Chief thought and then turned to his Sergeant. A moment later the office was in a frenzy of activity. Alyssa breathed a sigh of relief, her job was over. But maybe not.

"Can I come along?" The Chief looked at the model and thought of the force he was taking. It should be safe enough.

"Okay, Miss. But you'll ride with me."

Her head pounded and she could taste the blood trickling out of her mouth. The barrel of a rifle pushed into her back forced her forward, step after step over moorland. Every footfall was a struggle as there were little holes and pockets or just turf that gave way. Occasionally, she would have to climb up or jump down peat banks cut from the land, many left untouched for years.

Tommy kept coming to mind. She knew he would protect her from this man but also knew the danger she was taking his way. Part of her screamed to lead him away from any possibility of mermaids, tell him nothing, show him her inner steel. But the rifle point and a bullet through her heart was keeping her focused on heading to the shore. Her hope was that she was wrong about Tink, that she was stronger and had swum away.

The time had passed so quickly, in a whirlwind, from first eyeing Tommy up until Kiera had asked about the pool. But her feelings for him were strong, she knew this. Every time I'm around him I don't want to leave. I just want to be near, just want to enjoy him, she thought. And I want him to enjoy me. This can't be it. It's too soon to be over.

McCreedie told her to stop as they reached the water's edge. He looked down before asking her which way to go. Hayley nodded towards the east. She felt a harsh hand smack the back of her head.

"Don't lie to me. There's lots of footprints going west. You can haul that pretty butt over that way."

Now I'm in the dark, thought Hayley. Who knows how far along we have to go? They could be miles from here and this guy could be trigger happy before then. I'm going to need to do something. The rain was continuing and the going was slippery when Hayley had an idea. She saw a decent size branch up ahead, one which looked strong but manageable. Approaching it, she pretended to stumble before launching herself forward. Grabbing the branch, she managed to swing it round in one motion and strike it across McCreedie's hands.

The rifle fell to the floor and a shot rang out. The bullet struck a stone and disappeared harmlessly off into a nearby bush. Hayley tried to run but the same slippery ground gave way beneath her scrambling and she felt herself lifted up by the back of her shirt. Kicking out wildly with her legs had no effect as McCreedie pulled her up towards him and then grabbed her arms, holding them behind her.

"Pretty little thing ain't you?" he said looking her up and down. "You should learn your place, wench." Striking her with the back of his hand, he informed her that next time he'd make her take a swim in the loch, a permanent one. Given his actions, thought Hayley, that's where I am headed anyway.

They continued walking for another twenty minutes before she felt McCreedie reach round and grab her, holding a hand over her mouth. She listened, and yes, there were sounds up ahead. He must have good ears, thought Hayley. Apart from McCreedie's heavy breathing, she could hear men talking and one sounded like Tommy. Yes, it was Tommy. Her heart jumped and fell all at once. She was delighted and yet, he was now in danger.

McCreedie put Hayley back in front of the rifle and he prompted her forward with a nudge. Slowly, she walked and the heavy mist gradually dispersed. Kiera appeared from the mist sitting on a rock by the loch. Tommy was further back beside some men with Donald. And on the left in the loch were a plethora of mermaids, some with the smallest articles

she'd ever seen, nestled into their womanly chests.
"Bingo," laughed McCreedie.

# 25

# Mrs McKinney's Rescue

"Bloody hell, Mrs McKinney, you nearly took him out."

"Nearly is the operative word, James, young man, and kindly refrain from such expletives in my car."

"Kindly refrain from smacking anything else on the road then."

Afterwards, James would reflect on the many near misses and scrapes they had on the way to the loch and come to the opinion that Mrs McKinney was some divine angel sent down for the sole purpose of driving to people's rescue. Laura, on the other hand, didn't register most of these instances.

As they took the right angled bend towards the loch-side track, the rear end of the car slid out and James was flung hard down into the seat. Tutting to herself, Laura turned the wheel hard left and floored the accelerator one more time. The path now became rutted and slippery and James could only look straight ahead in terror. Careering down the hill at an ever increasing rate, Laura threw the car at each corner, fighting to straighten it afterwards.

With the fog that was still thick around the loch, Laura didn't realise how close to the edge she was and was caught by surprise on rounding a corner and seeing a young man hopping on the road. Laura slammed on the brakes but the car slid and the front end caught the man on the knee cap of his good leg. McCreedie's son spun round again before collapsing to the floor. Despite having struggled to hop up the track to the main road for help, he had been cut down a mere hundred yards from where Hayley had crashed. Tommy's car smashed against the tree, came into Laura's view. She was pumping the brakes to no avail and the car slid straight into the wreck.

Having been whipped forward by the accident, James had bounced back into the seat, his seat-belt performing admirably. It took a full minute for him to fully come to and realise the full extent of what had happened. Turning his neck slowly, he tried to see if his driver was alright. But Laura was missing.

Or rather she was in full flow back up the hill to address her victim. Rolling around in agony, young McCreedie was suddenly pinned down by an older woman kneeling onto his shoulders.

"Where's Kiera? You tell me now son, where is Kiera or God forgive me I'll do you a mischief?"

"Argggh! What...? Who....? What are you on about?" blurted the man.

"Kiera, the girl, where is she? Black hair? Slim, good looking. Where is she?"

"Who are you on about? Black hair? Black? She was blonde. Curvy. Big chest." Young McCreedie felt a slap across his face.

"Don't you speak so rudely. All you men think about. Apologise right now."

"You hit me with your car. You've smashed my kneecap. I bloody swear you've broke it."

"Language." Another slap to the cheek. "Where is she?"

"Dad took her. Down to the loch side. Down that way. Bloody hell, leave me alone. Get an ambulance you silly bitch." Slap! Slap! Slap! James arrived at the scene.

"You okay, Mrs McKinney?"

"She's fine. Just keep her away from me. The stupid bat's lost it." Slap!

"Young men today, just have no manners," accused Laura.

"Looks like he's in a bit of a mess," said James, "Did he say anything about Kiera?"

"Who the hell's Kiera?" shouted young McCreedie.

"Black hair, slim figure, good.....complexion?" said James with one eye on Laura.

"Blonde! I told the daft cow, she was blonde with big boobs." Slap!

"He said they went down to the loch," added Laura.

"Well we need to go down then, whoever has sent the message."

"What about this potty mouthed young man?"

"Get me an ambulance," shouted young McCreedie.

"I'll tie him up, the police shouldn't be too far behind."

James removed the young man's shoes and used his laces to tie his hands behind his back before dragging him to the side of the road. When he came alongside Laura, who had returned to her car, she was holding a poker in her hand.

"Where did you get that?"

"I was taking it to the charity shop but now it has a better use. My husband's in hospital, your girl has been harpooned, Kiera is in difficulty and there's a buxom blonde in trouble. It's time to end this nonsense." Without asking if he was coming along, Laura turned and walked downhill towards the loch-side. Left with no option James followed.

Laura covered the ground surprisingly quick for an older woman and James struggled to keep up, his senses reeling from the crash. Continuing as if the collision hadn't happened, Laura marched across the uneven ground until she got to the loch-side. The water was calm and everything seemed peaceful but the ground was disturbed with several sets of footprints.

"Look, Mrs McKinney, there's more footprints going this way. Do you think we should try this way first?" James' words were half lost as a rifle shot resounded from the mountains around the loch. Laura didn't even flinch as she turned and followed the greater footprint impressions. Defying her age, she started to break into a light jog, poker held high.

"Anyone does anything stupid and I'll blow a hole in you." Now with the barrel back between Hayley's shoulder blades, McCreedie radioed his colleagues. After giving his location, all he asked for was to bring the dynamite.

"Now then, if we can all come together and sit down just over there." Tommy walked slowly toward the rock McCreedie was pointing at, staring all the time at Hayley who was shaking with fright. Donald took Kiera's hand and led her to the rock. Coming closer, McCreedie pushed Hayley with the barrel into Tommy who grabbed her and held her close. "Just sit there and you'll be fine. All I want is the mermaids. Get rid of these bastard creatures once and for all."

"What have they ever done to you?" shouted Hayley. Tommy held her from jumping back up at the gunman.

"Killed my brother. On that boat in the harbour. Killed by that merman. Well that ain't enough to see him dead. Going to kill the lot. Before people get sentimental about these killers. Time to eradicate them. Stick of dynamite should be a start. Especially now they are hiding below.

The gunshot had made the mer-people dive but the occasional flipper and head could be seen popping up to the surface.

"Don't do this," begged Kiera, "they have young and mothers in there."

"All the better, we'll get them before they can breed again. Stop them before they start. Ah, my fellow hunters, I see you managed to subdue them. You," McCreedie said pointing at Tommy," take their bonds off. No messing or I'll blow blondie away."

Doing as instructed, Tommy received a punch across the jaw from the man he had hit with the rock. Containing his rage, Tommy returned to Hayley and held her, examining her face, and realised she had been struck several times. They're going to pay for this, thought Tommy, I'll rearrange his face.

"Once the lads are here with the dynamite, we'll sort these fish-ies out. No more trouble from them."

"What makes you think they're all in there anyway?" asked Kiera.

"Doesn't matter. Eye for an eye they say, isn't it? It'll be plenty more not to kill another fisherman."

Hayley bowed her head in Tommy's lap and wept. All my life I trained to help animals and he's just going to kill them right here in front of me. I can't watch, she thought, I can't.

During the next hour, Donald became more interested in some variations of colour he could see on the edge of his vision. Someone was on the move in the fog and they were being careful to stay just out of clear vision. They seemed to be scouting the area from what Donald could make out. He was sure there were at least two because their clothing seemed to be a different colour.

Continuing to watch the surrounds, Donald tried to look nonchalant as he did this. For the next half-hour the captives and the fishermen waited in an uneasy stand-off waiting for the other hunters to arrive. From out of the edges of the fog two men appeared, one carrying a rucksack and the other a rifle.

"Calum, is that it?"

"Yeah McCreedie, as requested. Twelve sticks in there. Where are the wee buggers anyway?"

"Gone down to the depths, though it can't be that deep here. Set the dynamite up. We'll fire it and launch it in from here. John," McCreedie said to the other man who had arrived and indicating Donald and his friends, "you keep your rifle trained on them. I don't want anyone disturbing this." McCreedie watched the preparations until he was satisfied. Taking one last glance at the captives and noting they were secure he slung his rifle over his shoulder and took the first stick.

"Calum, is the lighter ready?" Calum didn't answer but stared over McCreedie's shoulder. "I said, is it ready? What the hell's the matter with you?" Calum just pointed behind McCreedie who turned slowly to see a new arrival.

An older woman was slowly but deliberately making a line towards McCreedie. She appeared to be nonplussed by the guns held by the hunters and appeared unarmed.

"You sir, what do you think you're doing?" McCreedie blinked his eyes in disbelief. "I asked you a question, young man, now be soo good as to answer me."

"Who the hell's this?" asked McCreedie turning to his

compatriots. They shrugged. Laura continued to advance.

"Will you answer me, young man? Don't be so impertinent." Young man, thought McCreedie, I'm sixty. Getting to within three feet of the fisherman, Laura made an abrupt halt. "And guns, don't you realise people could get hurt, carrying on like that. What's that in your hand?"

"Dynamite." McCreedie wasn't sure why he had answered. It was like the lady expected an answer and so it produced itself from his mouth.

"Now that is dangerous. Didn't you ever read about those poor men in that mining disaster in '63? It's just not safe that type of explosive." This is silly, thought McCreedie, who does she think she is? Time to teach the damn busybody a lesson.

"Now listen here, Mrs do-gooder ...."

The poker struck him on the side of the head with surprising force for an older lady and McCreedie tumbled to the ground. Having come from behind Laura's back, he never saw the poker except for a brief glimpse in his peripheral vision but by then it was too late. The other captives and the fishermen were engrossed by the developments and hadn't spotted James coming close. As the poker was produced, he threw two large stones in quick succession at the other gun holders, striking one in the head, felling him, and the other on the arm so that his gun dropped.

As McCreedie fell, his gun, without the safety catch on, came off his shoulder and fired upon hitting the ground. The deafening shot caught Laura in the foot knocking her over. With chaos ensuing, Donald and Tommy grabbed their chance to jump on the other hunters and hand to hand fighting broke out. Kiera ran to Laura's aid while McCreedie rolled about on the ground holding his face.

Donald exchanged blows with Calum before diving at him and knocking him to the ground. Tommy and James were struggling to hold their own against larger opponents. Hayley tried to intervene but received a blow to her mid-riff for her pains. The fight was in the balance and blood had been drawn by both sides.

"Stand down, police! I said police! Stand down!" The harsh bark of the Chief constable broke through the fight and slowly the participants began to desist. Policemen started appearing at pace from all sides. "Everyone lie down on the floor with your hands behind your back, well away from your guns. No one make any aggressive moves. You are surrounded and you can't escape." Donald, Tommy, James and the other participants of the fight began to drop to their knees until another voice rang out.

"I don't think so Mr Policeman." All eyes turned to see McCreedie holding his cocked rifle at Kiera's head.

"Don't do anything stupid. No one has to get hurt here," advised the Chief Constable.

"That's where you're wrong, copper. You see there's a debt to be paid by some little fish-ies in this here loch. A family score to settle you might say, and this wench here is going to help me." McCreedie tapped Kiera's head with the rifle. "Nobody else move or she gets it."

"That'll be murder. You'll never get out for that."

"Well, there'll be no need if she does what she's told. You girl," he tapped Kiera's head again, "get the lighter." Slowly, Kiera moved to pick it up with McCreedie keeping the gun on her head all the time. Keep your head, Kiera told herself, keep your head. Her heart beat fast and her knees were quivering. Hold it together, I need to hold it together.

McCreedie's men, rather than step back into the breach, could start to see a wildness in his eyes. There was one thing to threaten and another to parade around with a gun in front of the cops. If anything happened, this would be cold blooded murder with no way out. The common sense in each of them said now was a time to remain clear of their leader. After all he was the leader, his idea. Honest, Mr Policeman, we were only after the mermaids.

Watching helplessly, Donald was torn in two between a dramatic dash to help or keeping a cool distance and preserving Kiera's life. So much had passed between them this last week and he just couldn't believe it could end here. He could see the fear in her, saw how her hands trembled, her knees shook. And as she caught his eye, her fear of losing him nearly broke him.

"Blondie, pick up the dynamite and follow us." Hayley, sniffing as tears overcame her again, slowly picked up sticks of dynamite until she could no longer carry any more. There were six in her hands. McCreedie, with Kiera at gunpoint led her onto a jutting rock some ten meters away. The rock was shaped so as to overhang the loch slightly and provided a good place to launch the dynamite from. Moving backwards up the rock with Kiera behind him, McCreedie placed himself at the edge.

"Give me a stick, Blondie," ordered McCreedie. Hayley couldn't look at him but offered a stick and then retreated.

"Don't do this," offered the Chief Constable one last time," they'll put you away for a long time."

"For killing mermaids, I doubt it, cop. Switch the lighter on, bitch." Kiera did as she was told and McCreedie leaned forward with the stick. The fuse lit and McCreedie straightened up to throw the dynamite. There was an eruption in the water as a merman leapt out and caught McCreedie's shoulder with a flick of its tail. Kiera felt the gun move off her head and took her chance. Driving her elbow backwards, and directly into McCreedie's manhood, Kiera let out a shriek as all her pent up tension was released with brutal force. McCreedie buckled, dropping the dynamite and fell backwards into the water. The water became violently agitated as fins and limbs could be seen repeatedly surfacing.

Running forward, Donald grabbed hold of the burning stick of dynamite as it toppled back towards the watching audience. Although it was his left hand, he instantly hurled the explosive which exploded some three seconds later before the dynamite had hit the ground. The force sent a few watchers to the ground but did no damage to any onlookers. Donald looked up to see a weeping Kiera running and then falling on top of him, clutching him tight, holding on for as if her life was still in the balance. He turned to look at her and she mouthed "I can't lose you."

"I know, Kiera, I know." Without giving a damn about anyone else, Donald took her in his arms frantically kissed her, before settling into a longer and deeper kiss. Kiera broke off, just as Donald was ready for another.

"Sorry, Laura's foot. I need to ... " Donald nodded and stayed putt as he watched Kiera race to Laura.

It was at least a minute, Tommy reckoned, before they could pull McCreedie from the water. He was battered, bruised and bleeding but alive unlike his brother. Hayley was clinging on like the end of the world hadn't just been averted. But Tommy didn't care. She was clinging on.

Breathing heavily, exhausted from the tension, the Chief

Constable scanned the scene in front of him. After calling for ambulances, placing an officer over the dynamite, sorting out the wounded and making sure the guns were disarmed, he took a moment to look at the now peaceful loch where the mer-people had resurfaced. They were swimming around, looking at the activity on the shore, some cradling small ones, others performing dives and somersaults. They were glorious, wonderful creatures, he thought. Then the vision of interviews, followed by paperwork, then the press conferences appeared before him. Bloody mermaids, he thought.

## 26

## Reflection

Fanning her face with a rolled up newspaper, Kiera sat beside the fire and watched Donald swimming in the sea. Mackerel spat and fizzed on the grill which occasionally sent a blast of smoke into her eyes. Sitting there, she realised her contentment, her peace with the world. After losing her friend nearly two years ago, she had reached a point of healing and one of the main balms had been Donald.

The time with the mermaid had changed him. No, thought Kiera, not changed, just brought his true self to the surface. She remembered how that night after McCreedie had fallen into the loch, Donald had taken her down to this very beach, away from all the hubbub and noise surrounding those fantastical creatures. It had been a cool night and she had shivered in his fleece as he dropped onto one knee. She had cried for joy and then laughed when he said, "let's do it tomorrow." But her eyes caught his and with a lump in her throat she realised he meant tomorrow.

How, where, who would be there? Kiera had peppered Donald with questions. And he said with Murdo. But what about her catholic folks back in Ireland. How would they accept a protestant wedding? So he had rung the priest at 6 a.m. The phone call remained with her. Donald pleading with a man still in his pyjamas. Then a whirl of activity and she was standing in the recovery ward side room, taking a ring upon her finger. Reverend McKinney and her priest presiding, Hayley with her bruised face and Alyssa with her painful shoulder, holding their bridesmaid's flowers. Tommy and James, standing with Donald and some nurses looking on, of which one rotund older lady was constantly in tears. And Laura, foot up in a wheelchair, just smiling and nodding her approval.

Donald's mother hadn't been impressed but she had attended the registry office when they had completed the civil part of the marriage. That had taken time and a little more formality but by then they were already a husband and wife, enjoying each other to the full, wondering how long this happiness could last. Well, it had lasted over a year.

Other things had changed since then. Kiera looked at Alyssa sat in the deck chair beside her with a parasol stuck in the ground, providing shade. Once an admired girl displaying her charms on various beaches for all to see, she still had her shirt open, exposed. But now there were two small human bundles finding their sustenance from their mother with an adoring father knelt at Alyssa's feet, fetching whatever she required for her motherly duties. After the mermaid excitement had died down, Kiera had been surprised that James and Alyssa had keep it going for they seemed to be from such different worlds. She had returned to modelling although everything was clothed now, her scar preventing any further glamour work. But she kept coming back to the island, or rather to James, and now they had set a home together.

"I didn't think they would make it." Kiera turned to see

Laura hobbling up to her. She had lost a few toes from the rifle shot and now had to use a crutch for balance. Sitting, she took Kiera's hand. "No, I put them down to part. Glad I was wrong."

"Her getting pregnant probably helped," replied Kiera.

"No, Kiera. If she hadn't have wanted him, the kids would have ripped them apart. She's found what she wants, and with her modelling still intact she's got to have her cake and eat it." Laura smiled.

"But you did help them. Giving her a place to stay when she was up. Helping her with the trauma. Does she still have the nightmares?"

"Oh yes, poor thing. But she copes. No, they cope." Laura turned away to look at her husband standing halfway down to the water's edge, looking out to sea.

"How is Murdo? It wasn't right what they did. I feel responsible."

"Stop that right now. He made his choice and I stood with him. If people can't accept these things it's their issue. He had every right to marry you."

"But they threw him out, Laura. After all he had done in that parish, they threw him out, just for letting Father McGinley give a blessing. I mean it's the same God, the same Jesus."

"I know Kiera. But not the same church. Not Jesus' church. But don't fret for Murdo. His trips to the mainland working on the streets of the capital have changed him. He's moving forward, closer to our God. That's what we want."

"But you lost your toes. You seem to have paid more than anyone for what happened."

"Nonsense Kiera, nonsense. I now write to McCreedie in prison and I'm visiting him in a fortnight. When would I ever have had the chance to be a friend to that man without all this? When? And look at your Donald. And you. So much good came from it. If there's been a price it's been worth paying. As they say, don't cry for me Argentina!" Laura stood and hobbled off towards Alyssa to coo over the children.

Kiera brooded over Laura's losses until she remembered about the war between the insurance company and Laura over the damage she had caused racing to the rescue. With the insurance company refusing to pay out because of her reckless driving, it had taken a local car sales company to come in and settle the accounts in return for Laura promoting the free driving lessons they were giving away with every new car. It had taken Laura some time and a forced arm to accept but James had found it all hilarious. He hadn't accepted a lift from Laura since that day. Kiera smiled at the idea.

"Hey, what's got you smiling?" Tommy sat down beside the fire and started poking at the fish. He received a slapped hand for his efforts.

"Get off, they're not ready." Kiera giggled at him. "Anyway I thought someone was back to slate your appetite."

Tommy stared down the beach at Hayley. Sitting right where the sea was coming in, she was allowing the water to run over her as it ebbed and flowed. Her hair was hanging loose and her bikini allowed for her back to be all but exposed, showing her curves. Tommy drank in the view.

"Well. Has it?"

"Has it what?"

"Been sated. Your appetite."

"It's been a while, I'll grant you that. When she got that offer from the American university for the research into the mermaids, I could see it was what she wanted," said Tommy with his head hanging low.

"Well she did take the lead in making sure they were protected. The whole protection program for the two months following the incident until they left, that was all her. And she learnt so much. It's no wonder they went for her. I mean, everyone wanted a piece of the mermaid action."

"I know, Kiera. But America was so far away. I mean look at her. She was over a year there. With that figure and her mind, she must have been in demand. And not just in lectures."

"But she convinced them to do research here, Tommy. She drove that. Hayley wants to be here. She wants to be with you."

"But things must have happened?"

"Why? Did anything happen with you? No, it didn't. And you know why. Take a leaf from Donald's book and get hold of her while you can. Stop pissing about Tommy before you lose her." As if, thought Kiera, Hayley was daft on the guy. Tommy looked straight at Kiera but his attention was elsewhere as if he was thinking out a problem. Then he just stood up and walked directly to Hayley to sit down beside her in the water. Donald was splashing about in front of them so Kiera, asking Laura to mind the food, shouted down to Donald. He waved and started towards her. She met him halfway to the water.

"What's up? Is it food time?"

"Donald, that stomach's going to grow." Kiera took his hand. "I just wanted to give them some space," she said nodding at the couple at the sea's edge. Donald stepped behind her and wrapped his arms round her waist, setting his chin on her shoulder. Together they looked out into the choppy expanse of water and both wondered the same thing.

"Where do you think she is, Kiera?"

"Tink'll be out there somewhere, some merman on her arm. Probably got a brood following her."

"Was weird when they left. Two months, all that media, and then just gone. Nothing really since. Not even a night time wave to the ferry."

"Someday they'll be back. And Hayley will be there to keep them safe. Work out how they live, how they get it on and where they keep the wee ones. They'll be back."

"And there'll be the same fiasco over them again. Are they human like us? Are they sentient? What can we do with them? It's never just beauty for beauty's sake, is it? We never appreciate, never wonder, just plan and use."

"How do you mean?"

"Well, take Alyssa, gorgeous girl but we want to objectify her. Same with the church. Never glory in it but instead use it for our purposes. And same with the mermaids. Make them a commodity, or make them a threat, for rallying people to our selfish ideas. I think Tink's better off out there."

"Probably. And besides Donald, I don't need you bringing any more naked women into my house." Donald laughed. "Do you think the fish smell will ever go from that bathroom?"

"I swear the pool still has a tinge and it's chlorinated," answered Donald.

"It turned out good, though Donald, didn't it? I mean there was a lot of nasty things happened but it did turn out okay?"

"Well, it could have been worse. All I know is I found my mermaid, who lured me in through the rocks, nearly broke my body on the way and who isn't going to give me up either." He kissed Kiera's neck and held her close.

"Looks like Tommy's been grabbed by a siren too." They watched Tommy on one knee staring up into Hayley's face.

She nodded and they cheered.

# More from the Author

Hopefully you dig these characters as much as I do in this window on island life. If I have intrigued you, mystified you, tickled you, or even offended you, then please check out my website and other author pages where all my scribings are laid out for your pleasure. Thanks for reading!

Website: www.grjordan.com
Twitter: @carpetless
Facebook: carpetlessleprechaun
Goodreads: G R Jordan
Email: gary@grjordan.com

Also check out the Austerley & Kirkgordon series, two misfits saving the world from mischievous paranormal intentions. All books available at Amazon and all good online and retail stores.

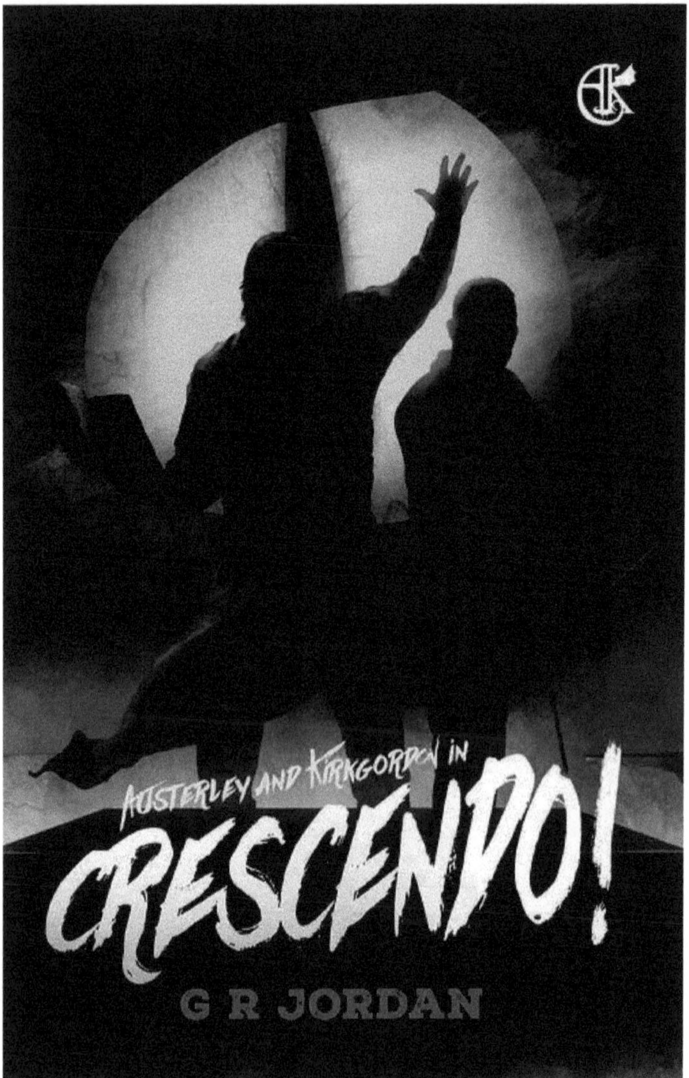
AUSTERLEY AND KIRKGORDON IN
CRESCENDO!
G R JORDAN

MORE FROM THE AUTHOR

## Austerley and Kirkgordon in THE DARKNESS AT DILLINGHAM

**G R JORDAN**

## SURFACE TENSIONS

# Acknowledgements

To Janet for her enthusiasm for my writing and giving me space to keep on knocking out the weird notions in my head.

To my wonderful children who let their Dad have some space and letting me be in their story.

To Chrisella, for your support and kind words!

To everyone who comments and feeds back on the initial workings I hand out, it makes it that much easier.

To Adrijus for the most excellent artwork. Check him out at rockingbookcovers.com.

To Kathleen and the Stornoway Writer's Group. Thanks for all the encouragement and honesty.

To God who gave me this creative talent, may I also use it to elucidate your world.

# Author Bio

G R Jordan is a self-published author who finally decided at forty that in order to have an enjoyable lifestyle, his creative beast within would have to be unleashed. His books mirror that conflict in life where acts of decency contend with self-promotion, goodness stares in horror at evil and kindness blind-side us when we at our worst. Corrupting our world with his parade of wondrous and horrific characters, he highlights everyday tensions with fresh eyes whilst taking his methodical, intelligent mainstays on a roller-coaster ride of dilemmas, all the while suffering the banter of their provocative sidekicks.

A graduate of Loughborough University where he masqueraded as a chemical engineer but ultimately played American football, Gary had worked at changing the shape of cereal flakes and pulled a pallet truck for a living. Watching vegetables freeze at -40'C was another career highlight and he was also one of the Scottish Highlands "blind" air traffic controllers. These days he has graduated to answering a telephone to people in trouble before telephoning other people to sort it out.

Having flirted with most places in the UK, he is now based in the Isle of Lewis in Scotland where his free time is spent between raising a young family with his wife, writing, figuring out how to work a loom and caring for a small flock of chickens. Luckily his writing is influenced by his varied work and life experience as the chickens have not been the poetical inspiration he had hoped for!

Lightning Source UK Ltd.
Milton Keynes UK
UKHW010642210820
368607UK00002B/444